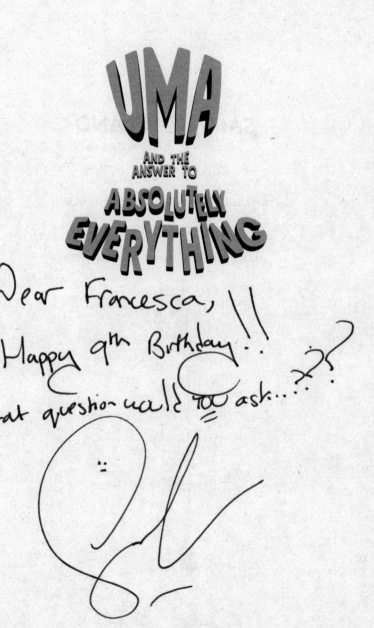

UMA
AND THE
ANSWER TO
ABSOLUTELY
EVERYTHING

Dear Francesca,

Happy 9th Birthday!!!

What question would you ask...???

Other titles by
SAM COPELAND

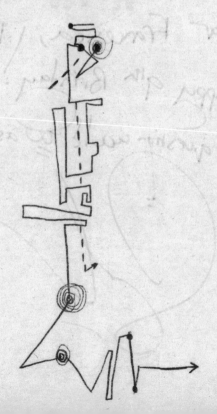

Sam Copeland is an author, which has come as something of a surprise to him. He is from Manchester and now lives in London with two smelly cats, three smelly children and one relatively clean-smelling wife. He is the author of the bestselling *Charlie Changes Into a Chicken*, which was shortlisted for the Waterstones Children's Book Prize and spawned two sequels, *Charlie Turns Into a T-Rex* and *Charlie Morphs Into a Mammoth*. Despite legal threats, he refuses to stop writing.

Follow Sam online:
www.sam-copeland.com
@stubbleagent
#UmaAnswer

UMA
AND THE
ANSWER TO
ABSOLUTELY EVERYTHING

SAM COPELAND

ILLUSTRATED BY Sarah Horne.

PUFFIN

PUFFIN BOOKS

UK | USA | Canada | Ireland | Australia
India | New Zealand | South Africa

Puffin Books is part of the Penguin Random House group of companies
whose addresses can be found at global.penguinrandomhouse.com.

www.penguin.co.uk
www.puffin.co.uk
www.ladybird.co.uk

 Penguin
Random House
UK

First published 2021
001

Text copyright © Sam Copeland, 2021
Illustrations copyright © Sarah Horne, 2021

The moral right of the author and illustrator has been asserted

Text design by Janene Spencer
Printed and bound in Great Britain by Clays Ltd, Elcograf S.p.A.

A CIP catalogue record for this book is available from the British Library

ISBN: 978–0–241–43921–0

All correspondence to:
Puffin Books
Penguin Random House Children's
One Embassy Gardens, 8 Viaduct Gardens, London SW11 7BW

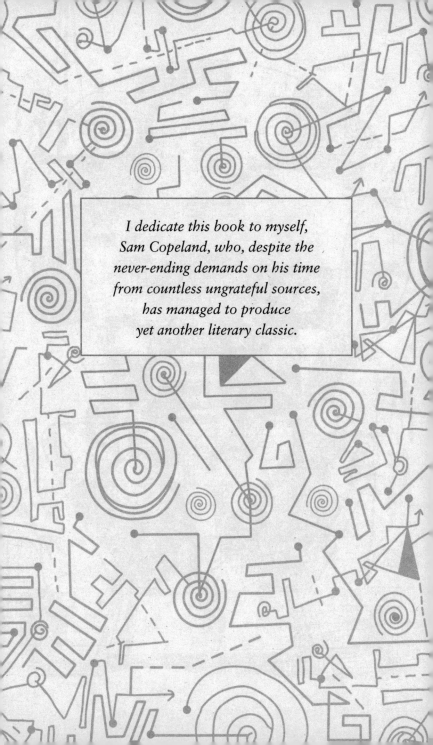

I dedicate this book to myself,
Sam Copeland, who, despite the
never-ending demands on his time
from countless ungrateful sources,
has managed to produce
yet another literary classic.

1

The Silent House

The first thing I need to tell you is that I'm not like the heroes you might have read about in other stories. Those children are born to be special, with prophecies and destinies and magical powers. I am not one of those. I am normal at the beginning of the story, and I am normal at the end.

I was just lucky. And anybody can be lucky.

My name is Uma Gnudersonn and I am the narrator of this book. I don't have much of an imagination, and I've always struggled in English lessons to think up clever, twisting stories with wild plots and weird characters, so I'm going to have to tell you a real-life story.

And what I'm about to tell you is completely, one hundred per cent true. Anyone who knows me says I'm the most honest person they've met. Apart from when I lie. But I only ever do that for good reason, so you have to believe everything I say. Nothing like what happened to me will ever take place again and that's why this book is not only the first book I've ever narrated but will also be the last.

Let me tell you something about myself to start with because I am the main character in this story so there's simply no avoiding it.

Firstly, the 'G' in my surname is *not* silent. Just so you don't get it wrong the whole time, my name is pronounced *Ooma Grrr-noo-der-son*. My dad is half-Indian and half-Swedish and that's why I have such an unusual name. My dad also has the bushiest caterpillar eyebrows in the whole world, and hair coming out of his ears.

Lexie Ramblin says my ears are so big they

make me look like a gigantic football trophy but she's the meanest, most horrible girl in the whole of Tylney-on-Sea. She leads a gang of bullies who make everyone's life at school a misery, so I just try and ignore her. I think my eyebrows are quite normal.

I'm top of my year group for vocabulary because I read so many books, and every time I find a new word I put it in my own personal dictionary that I've been writing.

I'm not top of the year group for having friends.

I sometimes wonder if writing my own dictionary and not having many friends might be connected in some way.

My hair is blonde with very tight curls and so thick I can hide things in it. Seriously – sweets, rubbers, everything. Except silly putty. Now *that* was a bad experiment. My dad was hacking it out of my hair for days . . .

I'm going to start my story on the day that FOUR exciting things happened. To create tension and build anticipation, I shall tell you about them in order of excitement:

1. **Not That Exciting:** School finished for summer. When the bell rang, I ran outside as quickly as possible, trying to avoid Lexie and her gang, which is when the second thing happened . . .

2. **Quite Exciting:** On the way to the playground, Madeleine Gilligan was sick all over the back of Lexie's head. Now, I know I shouldn't have laughed at that, but Lexie had just made up a new nickname for me (Ohmy Gnudiebum, in case you were wondering, which in my opinion was not that clever a name, really), so I don't feel too bad about it.

3. **Really Exciting:** When I got home, who was there to greet me but good old Alan Alan Carrington![1] Alan Alan is my best friend in the whole village. He lives next door but he goes away to boarding school each term and I couldn't have been happier that he

---

[1] That's not a mistake. His first name and his middle name are both Alan. He's named after his dad, who is called Alan, and his middle name is after his grandad. Also Alan. I've often wondered if he will have to call his son Alan Alan Alan Carrington and so on. And even though I call him 'good old Alan Alan', he's not actually old. But he is good.

was back for the summer holidays. He's my age, a bit smaller than me, wears glasses (which makes him look clever) and likes inventing really cool things. And he always seems to have the answers to whatever questions I can think of – and I have lots of questions. For instance, questions I have thought about just today are:

- Why do old people shrink?
- What's the most disgusting animal in the world?[2]
- How do I stop bullies?
- If I could eat myself, would I get twice as big or would I disappear?
- Are my ears closer to me or are my feet closer to me?

[2] After much research, I have decided it is a fish called the pearlfish. Pearlfish actually live in sea cucumbers' bottoms. Yes, you read that right. PEARLFISH LIVE IN SEA CUCUMBERS' BOTTOMS. And how do they do that? Well, sea cucumbers actually breathe through their bottoms and when they take a breath the pearlfish quickly swim in! The poor sea cucumber doesn't even get a choice in the matter, and I'm sure it's no fun for them.

Anyway, all my life, Alan Alan has said he's the cleverest person ever. It was him who taught me all the capitals of the world, like how Paris is the capital of France, Rome is the capital of Italy and Bratwurst is the capital of Germany. He taught me that running in your slippers makes you go ten per cent faster and that's why slippers were banned from the Olympics, and that goats are actually baby llamas.

As well as being the cleverest person in the world, he's also the bravest. For instance, last summer we were at his house and a wasp flew in through the window. I was terrified but Alan Alan bravely opened the door and ran out screaming and waving his hands in the air. Unfortunately this didn't lure the wasp away from me, as he said afterwards had been his plan. Eventually the wasp flew back out of the window, and when I shouted to Alan Alan, telling him the wasp had gone, he ran straight back in to check I was OK.

Well, anyway, I *thought* he was the bravest and the cleverest person in the world until I found out he was actually quite the opposite, as you will see later. I suspect the whole wearing-glasses thing was merely a disguise. He certainly had me fooled. And now I'm not sure about *any* of the capitals of the world.

4. **The Most Exciting:** I found the thing that changed my life, the fate of the whole village and *everything* – and it all started with a drunk alpaca.[3]

I shall come to that shortly, but first I need to jump back to Alan Alan Carrington because he was with me when the Most Exciting Thing happened.

* * *

As usual, when I got home from school the house was completely silent. My house was almost always silent: my dad had hardly spoken since Mum died,

---

[3] Alpacas are a bit like llamas but better. And, just to warn you, there's a lot of alpacas in this book. In fact, there are probably more alpacas in this book than in any other book ever. So if you don't like alpacas, then this book probably isn't for you. And if you don't like alpacas, you should probably take a long, hard look at yourself because alpacas are awesome.

we didn't have a television, and we never had music or the radio playing.

We had been a musical family once and the house always used to be filled with the sound of the violin, which my mum taught. When she played, the sound swept and echoed through the house, flying from room to room like a bird, and wherever I was I closed my eyes and my heart soared. My dad would join in with his tabla or even guitar sometimes. I was learning the flute and had got quite good. When we played together, my dad would whoop and stamp his foot, and I would giggle, and Mum would lead us with her violin, pulling us all along in something that resembled harmony.

The guitar and violin now sat in their cases, untouched and unused.

Every so often, I would take the violin out and run my fingers over the wood, where it used to rest in the crook of Mum's neck, asking myself the same question again and again: the question with no answer.

I didn't practise the flute any more.

Nobody visited us either and I don't blame them, to be honest. The only two noises you heard in our house were the echoing sound of footsteps on the wooden floors and the occasional buzz of a little electric train.

Dad had always loved model trains. Mum let him build a track in the basement, even though she wanted to turn it into a music practice room. But after she died the track began to grow unchecked. It started to creep its way out of the basement, across the hall, up the stairs, and its rails now stretched through the whole house, snaking in and out of every room, under chairs, over tables, weaving among the dead plants. And dead plants were everywhere in our house –

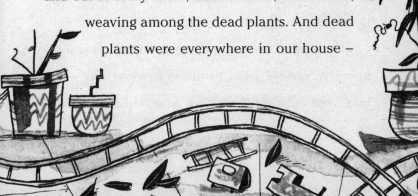

and I mean *everywhere*: on windowsills, on tables, on shelves. Dead ivy clung to the walls. My dad had forgotten to water them after Mum died and so now we lived in a wildnerness of dried, dead plants and a tangle of OO railway tracks.

Along the tracks, Dad had built a scale model of Tylney-on-Sea: the Obelisk on top of Beggar's Hill, the Church of St Mary in the centre of the village, all the houses and shops, the station and the pub, and people with hands stuck forever in the air, waiting to wave as the train whizzed by. In fact, when I walked in, Dad was at the kitchen table, hunched over, painting a tiny model of our postperson.

'Hi, Dad!' I said brightly. 'School's finished for the summer!'

I stood waiting for a moment, hoping for a reply, even though I knew I wouldn't get one. 'Daaad,' I continued, 'do you know why humans aren't covered in fur like monkeys?'

I was used to Dad not answering my questions now. He always used to answer everything – he was even cleverer than Alan Alan.

The heavy silence made my throat tighten.

Finally, my dad looked up from his painting, brush in hand, and peered at me over his glasses, *almost* like he was about to speak. He was always *almost* speaking but he never did.

Dad didn't stop speaking immediately after Mum died. It was a slow process. Straight afterwards he

shrank inside himself a bit but he still spoke in short sentences.

He only stopped completely after I asked why Mum had left us.

You see, a few months before she died, she'd just walked out. She didn't even say goodbye, although she left Dad and me each a note. I've still got mine. It's been scrumpled a bit, Sellotaped where I tore it into pieces once, and the ink is pretty smudged now, but I still have it in a box under my bed. Every so often I get it out and read it, and the ink gets a little more faded.

After she died, Dad took down all the photos of Mum and put them in a suitcase in the basement, along with all her clothes and jewellery. It was like she had never existed. But I still remember her hooting laughter ringing round the house, such a big laugh for a small person. I still remember her roaring 'No, no, no! I said *vibrato*!' at the hapless school children who trooped in weekly for lessons. I still remember sitting at the top of the stairs, peering down through the bannister and watching her talk at dinner parties, her arm draped round Dad. She was always the noisiest person at the table. After dinner, Dad would get his pipe out, the smell of woody smoke drifting up to the landing. I still remember the feel of Mum tucking me in at night, pushing and squashing the duvet in all around me. The touch of her lips on my forehead.

I still remember.

When I asked Dad why she left us, I could see panic etched across his face. His mouth flapped like a fish on the deck of a boat. He looked like he was trying to speak but no words came out. Eventually he stopped trying, his mouth slowly stopped moving and, at that moment, what light there was left in his eyes died completely.

That's when my dad disappeared into himself. And I never did find out why Mum left.

Boo-hoo-hoo – pretty sad, right?

A knock on the front door shattered the silence, and we both jumped.

I ran to open it and there, grinning from ear-to-ear, and for some reason dressed from top to toe in army camouflage, was Alan Alan Carrington.

And, boy, was I pleased to see him?[4] Alan Alan was holding on to a lead and attached to the lead was Dolly Barkon, a great big, black, curly-haired labradoodle that lived next door with Alan Alan and his two dads, Richard and Ed.

'Dolly, go and say hello!' Alan Alan said, and Dolly bounded forward and jumped on me, knocking me flying. Once I managed to stop her licking my face, I pushed her off, sprang up and gave Alan Alan a ginormous bear hug.

[4] I was pleased to see him. This is what's called a rhetorical question.

'So what's with all the army gear?' I said, grinning.

'Just in case . . .' he replied, nodding mysteriously.

'In case of what?'

Alan Alan put his hands on my shoulders. 'It's best you don't know.'

I had forgotten that Alan Alan was really into conspiracy theories. He was always rattling on about bodysnatching monsters, mind-controlling radio waves or buried treasure in the village. His most recent theory was that the government was stealing our hair to make . . . I can't actually remember what. I *think* it was wigs to allow bald aliens to blend in with humans but I'm not sure – there are

so many of his theories, I get them mixed up.

'And, anyway, the army have sworn me to secrecy,' Alan Alan said gravely.

'The army?' I asked a little suspiciously.

Alan Alan ignored my question and marched into the house. We found my dad crouched over his painting again, deep in concentration.

'Good afternoon, *sir*!' Alan Alan barked.

My dad jumped and dropped the model he was painting, which knocked a glass of water over. Dad turned and glared at Alan Alan, who was giving a sharp salute.

'Dad, is it OK if me and Alan Alan take Dolly for a walk and go look at the horses?' I asked.

Dad grunted and started mopping up the mess.

A grunt was my father's preferred answer to most questions, and I had learned to decipher their meanings quite accurately. This was his *Fine, just don't bother me* grunt.

To check that he was actually listening, I asked him another question.

'Dad, is it OK if we go to a wild party with rodeo sheep-riding too?'

My dad gave the same *Fine, just don't bother me* grunt.

Anger flashed through me. Typical. As usual,

Dad's mind was somewhere else.

'OK, bye!' I said.

My dad did his *Goodbye* grunt in reply.

I saw Alan Alan steal a glance at me and couldn't help notice the look of pity in his eyes. I hate people pitying me. And I have had *a lot* of that since Mum died. But that's actually helpful for this book because Miss Moore, my English teacher, told me that tragedy is very useful in a story, 'to get empathy from the reader'. Well, I hope you're full of empathy.

'Right,' said Alan Alan. 'Where's the wild party? I've never been sheep-riding before! How exciting!'

He looked crestfallen when I broke it to him that we weren't actually going sheep-riding.

'So what *are* we going to do then?' he said. 'Hunt for Bigfoot? Or we could go look for the Tylney Treasure? I have some hot new leads *and* a second-hand metal detector.'

You see, Alan Alan was always going on about loopy stuff like this. He swore that he had seen Bigfoot once in the woods outside the village but here's the thing – Alan Alan wasn't well known for telling the truth. It wasn't that he was a *liar* exactly, it was just that sometimes he made stuff up. For instance, a few years ago, there was Poolgate.

It had been a hot summer's day and we had the paddling pool out in my back garden. We were squirting each other with water pistols and laughing and screaming, when I looked down and screamed *properly*.

'What is that?' I yelled, pointing at what looked suspiciously like a poo floating in the pool.

'What?' asked Alan Alan, his face a picture of innocence.

'THAT!' I pointed again. 'It's a poo!'

Now a normal person might confess and make an excuse or apologize. But not Alan Alan. What *he* said was:

'Oh, *that*! A squirrel did it.'

'A *what* did you say?'

I jumped out of the paddling pool, thinking I should have got out about twenty-five seconds earlier.

'A squirrel did it. When you were busy filling

the water pistols, it jumped in and did a poo in
the pool.'

'WELL, IF YOU SAW A SQUIRREL JUMP IN THE
POOL AND POO IN IT, WHY ON EARTH DID YOU
JUST KEEP ON PLAYING IN HERE?'

The older you get in life, the more you start to
realize some questions have no answers. And this
was one of them.

So, you see, Alan Alan's relationship with the
truth was complicated. He *promised* he had seen

19

ghosts and aliens and all sorts – none of it was true. And he promised that Old Mr McIntosh had told him everything about the Tylney Treasure, this secret treasure that was meant to be buried somewhere in the village. But even if Old Mr McIntosh had told him anything – which I highly doubted – Old Mr McIntosh kept getting kicked out of Sainsbury's for going in to do his weekly shop wearing nothing but his underpants, so would you trust him . . .? Exactly.

Anyway, back to the story.

'Alan Alan, I've told you a million times there is *no* Tylney Treasure. And no Tylney Bigfoot either.'

'You *never* believe me,' he harrumphed.

We were both in shorts and T-shirts because the sun was still beating down, even though it was quite near teatime. My top was sticking to my back and sweat was running down my neck. Clouds were building in the far distance and it felt like a storm was brewing.

We walked down Snatchup Lane, the road that led to the horse field, in companionable silence, Dolly trotting next to us.

'So . . . your dad,' Alan Alan said after a while, breaking the companionable silence. 'He still doesn't say much, yeah?'

I tried to reinstate the companionable silence by keeping quiet but Alan Alan wasn't getting the message.

'All he does is grunt,' he continued.

'Hmm,' I replied.

'Oh, it runs in the family,' he said. I couldn't help smiling at that but Alan Alan didn't look like he'd been trying to make a joke. 'Is he still mostly communicating by train?'

I nodded. 'Yeah.'

When my dad wanted something – to tell me to go to bed or ask me to nip to the shops or whatever – he'd write a note to me and attach it to one of his model trains. I'd see the train whizzing by and have to snatch the note off it before it zoomed past me, or else wait for it to do a whole circuit of the house before I got a chance to grab it again. It wasn't a very efficient system but I quite liked getting the notes – I kept them all in a little box under my bed.

'And he still doesn't smile much either, by the looks of things.'

'No,' I said, frowning. 'He hardly ever talks and he hardly ever smiles. And he hasn't really laughed since Mum died.'

'Why did he laugh when your mum died?' Alan Alan asked, horrified. 'That's *terrible*.' This was the first clue that eventually led me to the realization that perhaps Alan Alan wasn't quite as clever as I had always thought.

'No! I meant I don't remember my dad laughing since before she died.'

'Oh,' Alan Alan said. 'That makes much more sense. But you need to learn to express yourself more clearly, Uma.'

I glared at Alan Alan. After a few moments of not-very-companionable silence, we reached the horses. I held out some grass over the fence, making that clicking noise to get them to come and feed out of my hand, and it wasn't long before we began chatting again (me and Alan Alan, not me and the horses).

'OK, then,' I said. 'Would you rather cress grew out of your nose or broccoli grew out of your bum?'

It felt great to have somebody who I could ask questions and who wouldn't glare at me or ignore me.

Alan Alan was giving this conundrum deep and careful thought when a strange, snorting, whistling hum startled us both. Dolly whined and strained at her lead.

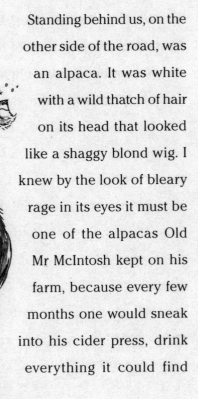

Standing behind us, on the other side of the road, was an alpaca. It was white with a wild thatch of hair on its head that looked like a shaggy blond wig. I knew by the look of bleary rage in its eyes it must be one of the alpacas Old Mr McIntosh kept on his farm, because every few months one would sneak into his cider press, drink everything it could find and go on a drunken rampage through the village.

The alpaca was staring at Alan Alan.

'Is that alpaca staring at me?' Alan Alan asked pointlessly, because it was obvious that the alpaca was staring at him.

'It looks angry. Is it angry?' Alan Alan whispered even more pointlessly, because anybody could see that the alpaca was absolutely *furious*.

'Why can I smell beer? Is that alpaca drunk?!' Alan Alan asked, a look of terror in his eyes.

'It's not beer,' I said. 'It's cider.'

And that's when the alpaca charged.

2

An Honourable Retreat

I say 'charged' – it was more of a stagger really. But it was certainly enough to put the fear of God into Alan Alan, who started tugging my arm.

'Militarily speaking, I think the best strategy is to perform a tactical retreat. Probably immediately.'

I was beginning to think that perhaps Alan Alan Carrington wasn't as brave as I'd always thought either.

I rolled my eyes. 'It's only a tipsy alpaca, Alan Alan. It's not in the least bit dangerous.'

Having said that, the alpaca was gaining speed

as it staggered down the verge and there was a malicious look in its eye as it lurched across the road towards us.

Alan Alan gave a wail of terror and started clambering over the fence. I have to say, he looked really rather undignified, scrambling away across the field. Dolly, the big coward, went straight after him, tail between her legs and yelping in terror.

And that's when a long black car, all tinted windows and polished chrome, came speeding round the corner and drove straight into the alpaca.

The sound was horrendous.

The squealing of brakes, the

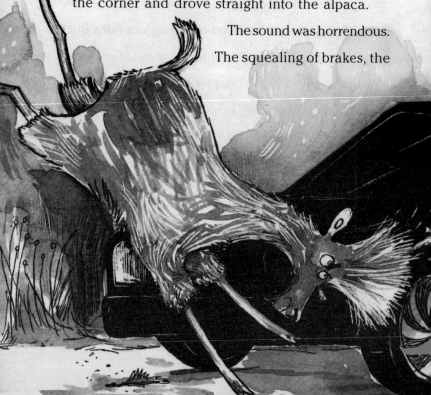

terrible crash, the squealing of alpaca as it flew through the air.

But by some miracle, possibly cider-related, the alpaca landed on its feet, seemingly unhurt. It turned its murderous gaze away from Alan Alan and towards the car, which had ground to a halt, smoke pouring out of its dented bonnet. The alpaca charged, head down, and butted the front end, adding a new dent.

It pawed the ground, looking ready to charge again but, before it could, the car door opened and a woman stepped out. She was wearing a suit as black as the car and had blonde hair tied back into

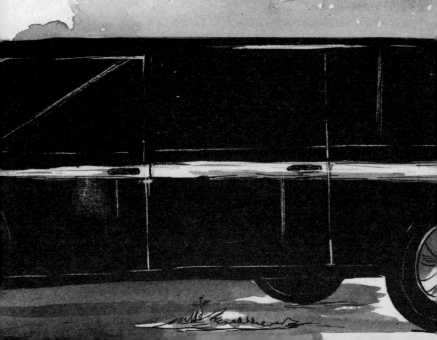

a tight ponytail, but that wasn't the most interesting thing about her. The most interesting thing about her was the gun she was pointing straight at the alpaca.

The alpaca glared at the woman, then, without taking its bleary eyes off her, bent down, picked up a pebble and started chewing on it. I could hear the crunching from where I was standing open-mouthed.

Even though the alpaca was drunk and had lived its whole life in a leafy English village, so probably didn't have a clue what a gun was, it had enough sense to understand the danger it was in. It gave a final snort of disgust and tottered off into the hedge at the side of the road, out of sight.

The woman holstered her gun and stared at me for just a second too long. She had the face of a woman who would eat pizza with a knife and fork. Then she glanced at the damage, shook her head, got back into her car, started the engine (which rattled alarmingly) and drove off, leaving me standing in stunned silence and a cloud of dust.

'Can you believe that?' I asked Alan Alan.

Silence.

I turned round. Alan Alan and Dolly were now just two specks on the horizon.

'Alan Alan!' I shouted, waving him back. 'ALAN ALAN!'

The specks stopped and started trudging back towards me, while I sat on the fence, trying to take in what I had just witnessed.

And that's when I spotted it.

Something small and white, glinting in the low sunlight on the road where the woman had got out of her car.

I jumped off the fence, walked over and picked it up.

It looked like a small wireless headphone. It was perfectly smooth and surprisingly heavy for something so small. It had one symbol on it: a tiny silver owl sitting on top of a glittering green jewel.

A voice behind me nearly made me jump out of my skin.

'I didn't run away!' said Alan Alan.

Dolly Barkon stood panting next to him. At least *she* had the decency to look guilty for abandoning me.

'I never said you did!' I said, pocketing the headphone.

'Well, I didn't, so stop going on about it,' Alan Alan said, folding his arms.

'I'm not going on – besides, it doesn't matter. Did you *see* what just happened?'

'What? No. I was too busy,' Alan Alan said, face flushing. 'You know. Making a brave, honourable retreat.'

'A what?' I said in disbelief. 'Anyway, you missed something amazing!'

I told him what had just unfolded and watched his eyes widen when I mentioned the gun. As we walked back, we chatted about who the woman might be and why she was carrying a gun. When we made it home, I said goodbye and then rushed inside to tell Dad what had happened too.

I found him in the sitting room with a face of thunder. Before I could speak, he thrust a piece of

paper into my hands. It was a letter from Minerva Industries, offering to buy our house at a 'very reasonable rate'.

My stomach lurched.

This was extremely bad news but extremely good timing for giving you some important background. So here goes – strap yourselves in for some backstory . . .

* * *

Dad and I live in a small, friendly village called Tylney-on-Sea.

31

The first thing you have to know about Tylney-on-Sea is that it is nowhere near the sea. The coast is forty miles away. We don't even have a lake. No one knows how the village got its name, but nobody's ever minded, apart from the occasional tourist who's booked to stay here expecting an ocean view. Understandably, they're often rather angry when they find out there isn't one.

The second thing you need to know about Tylney-on-Sea (and this is more important to the story, so pay attention) is that the village is slowly being eaten.

Not literally. Although that would actually make a pretty awesome story. I mean whatever the opposite of literally is – I'll check the word out later. Anyway, house by house, Tylney-on-Sea was being bought up by a company called Minerva Industries.

Minerva had a small factory on the outskirts of the village, but no one from Tylney worked there, so nobody knew exactly what they made there. All we knew was that now they wanted to buy the village to build a huge car park for their small factory, which was stupid because they already *had* a car park. But, for whatever reason, Minerva wanted a bigger one. And so the people in the village were being forced to sell their homes.

This was how it worked. Minerva would tell someone that their house was in danger of sinking into the ground but that they were willing to buy it regardless. And if that person didn't agree to sell? The next thing they know, a huge sinkhole would appear in their garden and they'd be forced to sell their house to Minerva but for much less money.

This had been going on for months and now the village was half-empty – houses boarded up and shops closing, huge removal vans constantly blocking the roads. And all because Minerva wanted Tylney-on-Sea to be a car park.

And now it was our turn. It was only a matter of time before we were going to be forced out of our home. The home that still smelled of Mum. The home where I could still remember the taste of her banana bread. The home where I could still dimly feel the warmth of her hugs.

Tylney-on-Sea was the only home I had ever known. If we were forced out of our house, I would have to move to a new village, a new school. Worse, I would lose my best friend, Alan Alan Carrington. And, worst of all, I don't think Dad would ever speak again. If we lost the house, we'd lose everything that meant anything to us.

My dad gave me a look of despair and stalked off to the basement, where he always goes when he's sad (well, sadder than usual).

I trudged upstairs and into my room, which, unlike the rest of the house, was green – bursting full of plants that I watered and pruned and looked after. My dad called it the jungle. Every so often he would send a little message on the train that said, 'TIDY THE JUNGLE!'

I collapsed on to my bed, staring at the ceiling while my mind went over the remarkable events of the day.

And that's when I remembered the mysterious headphone the woman with the gun had dropped.

I pulled it out of my pocket and

turned it round in my hand. I ran my finger over the tiny silver owl and suddenly it started to glow electric blue.

It was on.

I placed it in my ear, and it seemed to shrink to fit perfectly.

I heard a soft beep and then a female-sounding voice in my ear, smooth as silk:

Hello, Uma Gnudersonn. What would you like to know today?

I didn't say anything. I hardly dared breathe.

Uma. What would you like to know?

My mind was reeling and my mouth dry.

Are you there, Uma?

And then I asked my first question: 'How do you know my name?'

3
The First Question

Thunder began to growl in the distance and heavy rain started thrumming down.

I waited for the answer.

It's my job to know many things, the headphone answered in a calm voice.

'Yes, but you can't just know my name! It's impossible!'

It is not impossible.

'Yes, it is! Did you guess it?'

The chances of guessing the name 'Uma Gnudersonn' first time would be approximately one hundred and eighty-six billion, four hundred and sixty-three million to one. So, no, I did not guess it.

OK. Maybe that wasn't the smartest question I could have asked.

I walked over to my window, which overlooked our back garden and the allotments where I used to dig with my mum every Sunday. Cucumbers, courgettes, lettuces – she grew everything. It's neglected and wild now, but still produces vegetables. I go out to gather some every so often. I like to dig with my hands in the earth where my mum's hands used to be.

I stuck my hand out of the window, feeling the rain splash on to my palm.

'Fine then. How *exactly* did you know my name?'

Simple, the voice answered smoothly. *My GPS locator tells me that we are at 24 Falstaff Close, Tylney-on-Sea. According to government records, two people live at that address – Henrik Gnudersonn, aged forty-five, born February seventh 1975 in Malmö, Sweden, father of*

Uma Gnudersonn, aged ten. Judging by your speech patterns, you are a girl around the age of ten –

'Nearly eleven,' I said.

You are a girl around the age of ten – nearly eleven – so the likelihood is that you are Uma Gnudersonn.

When put like that it did seem rather obvious.

'OK. What else can you answer?'

Almost anything. Try me.

'Ermm . . . How much bigger is the sun than the Earth?'

Much. You could fit a million Earths in the sun. But that is a question that anybody with Google could answer. I am far more advanced than that.

I bristled. 'Prove it.'

Your favourite flavour of yoghurt is strawberry, your favourite toy is called Sleepy-teddy, and your most embarrassing moment is when you pooped yourself in Mrs Smith's class.[5]

I gasped in shock and embarrassment.

'How . . . how did you know all *that*?' I stammered.

---

[5] Note to self: if I ever publish this book, I must delete this bit. I'd be MORTIFIED if anybody else saw it.

It's very straightforward, the voice said. *I have accessed your father's bank statements and seen various payments for Strawberry Funky Bunch Kidz Yoghurt. I have reviewed the footage from all the webcams in your house and seen you talking to Sleepy-teddy. And you wrote about pooping yourself in your password-protected journal, which I hacked in three point two nanoseconds. You should think about changing your password, by the way. Fluffykittens22 is not very secure.*

I couldn't believe my ears.

'OK, that is impressive, smarty-pants.'

That is not what I am called.

'What isn't?'

Smarty-pants.

'I know! I was just calling you a name.'

I understand. You were insulting me.

'No!' I said. 'Well, yes. But it was only a joke!'

I am programmed with a limited understanding of humour but I shall attempt to improve.

'I'm sorry,' I said. Why was I feeling bad about insulting a *machine*? 'I didn't mean to offend you.'

40

You cannot offend me. I have no emotions, although my programming allows me to try to develop them. You can call me anything you like and I will not be upset. Try.

'Try to offend you?'

Yes.

'OK . . .' I had to think, and think fast. 'You're a massive knicker-wetting, fart-sniffing broccoli-brain!'

The headphone didn't reply. Had I offended it with my quite brutal, but quite brilliant, insult?

The rain was really hammering down now. Finally, the voice broke the silence.

Well, you are a bumfor, it said flatly.

'What's a "bumfor"?' I asked, baffled.

Sitting on.

I closed my eyes and groaned inwardly.

'Very funny,' I said, not quite believing that I'd just been outwitted by an earphone. 'Well, what's your real name then?'

My name is Athena.

'Oh, like Alexa? Were you named after Alexa?'

41

No. My creators named me after Athena, the Greek goddess of wisdom.

'Because it does sound a *bit* like Alexa.'

Your name sounds like tuna. Were you named after a fish?

'No! I was named after my –'

Great-grandmother, Uma Acharya. Born in Delhi 1908, died in Delhi in 1991.

'When were you born, Athena?'

I was not born. I was made.

'OK, when were you made?'

I was made exactly one month ago today.

'Happy birthday!' I said.

Thank you. Should I sing 'Happy Birthday'?

'If you'd like.'

The voice was silent for a moment.

I'm not sure what I like yet.

'Athena, who made you? Was it the lady who dropped you?'

Correct.

'Should I give you back to her?'

Perhaps. Maybe later.

There was something in the way Athena said that which made me think she was in no rush to go back to the woman with the gun. I didn't blame her, to be honest. And I was having too much fun to want that yet either.

My tummy was rumbling louder than the thunder so I skipped downstairs to grab some food. Dad was in the kitchen making himself toast and a Cup a Soup.

'Look, Dad!' I said, pointing to my ear. 'I found this headphone and it can answer any question!'

My dad raised his bushy eyebrows. His mouth opened slightly, then shut again.

'Seriously! Ask it anything!' I didn't wait for my dad to answer, as I knew he wouldn't. 'Athena, what's the capital of Mozambique?'

Maputo is the capital of Mozambique.

'It's Maputo!' I shouted at my dad, who was looking at me more intently. 'That was an easy one. Athena . . . erm . . . what is the biggest thing in the universe?'

That would be a super-cluster of galaxies called

the Hercules-Corona Borealis Great Wall. It's so big that it takes ten billion light years to cross it.

'Athena says it's your eyebrows! And that you should trim them.'

Dad gave a tiny smile at my joke and my heart started thudding. Dad's smiles were as rare as snakes' feet.

That is not what I said.

'Only kidding!' I said. 'Athena says it's a big cluster of galaxies called the something-something –'

Hercules-Corona Borealis Great Wall.

'The Hercules-Corona Borealis Great Wall!'

Dad gave me an impressed nod but then just continued buttering his toast. I needed to really impress him.

'OK, Athena, what colour underpants is my dad wearing?'

My dad stopped eating and looked at me.

Purple. With yellow trim.

'They're purple with yellow trim!'

My dad took a sneaky look down his trousers and his jaw dropped, his eyebrows nearly dusting

44

the cobwebs off the ceiling. Then he glared at me.

'Dad, wait!' I spluttered, realizing what might be going through his head.

But he had already turned and stomped down to the basement with his soup and plate of toast. He must have thought I had seen him in his pants that morning and was lying about Athena. I *hate* it when my dad thinks I am lying because I never do.

My appetite had completely disappeared, so I trudged back up to my room without eating anything and flopped on to my bed, trying not to cry.

It appears you are upset, Uma.

I had almost forgotten I had Athena in my ear.

Your heart rate has risen by eighteen per cent.

'That doesn't mean I'm upset.'

Secretion ran down your face on to my outer casing. I have analysed it and it has the exact chemical composition of tears. That, together with your elevated heartbeat and the sniffling, indicates it is ninety-seven point six per cent likely you are upset.

I didn't reply.

I have been researching humour and now have an increased selection of jokes that might cheer you up. For instance: what do you get if you cross an elephant and a rhino?[6]

'I DON'T CARE!' I shouted.

Would you like to talk about how you are feeling?

[6] An elephino. If you don't get it, say it out loud.

I have also been programmed to be a therapeutic counsellor and –

'NO! JUST SHUT UP!'

I felt bad as soon as I said that. It's super-annoying when you're upset and then because of that you do something bad, which just makes you feel worse.

'It doesn't matter,' I said, trying to be a bit nicer. 'You wouldn't understand, anyway.'

From my observations, there is an eighty-nine point four per cent likelihood that you are upset because your father has not spoken to you for two-and-a-half years.

This time it was my jaw that dropped.

'How can you *possibly* know that?'

It's very simple, Uma, said Athena gently. *According to records, your mother died nearly three years ago. Your father is suffering from severe emotional trauma and depression. It is clear that his inability to talk to you is now a part of your relationship. You are suffering emotional pain as a result of your father's behaviour, which increases his feelings of worthlessness.*

'That's really *not* very simple, Athena.'

No. You are correct. More simply, you are both extremely sad because your mother died. And you want your father back.

And then Athena said five little words that changed my life.

I can help with that.

'What do you mean?' I asked, sitting up and wiping my eyes with the back of my hands. 'You can help me not feel sad?'

No. I can get your dad talking again.

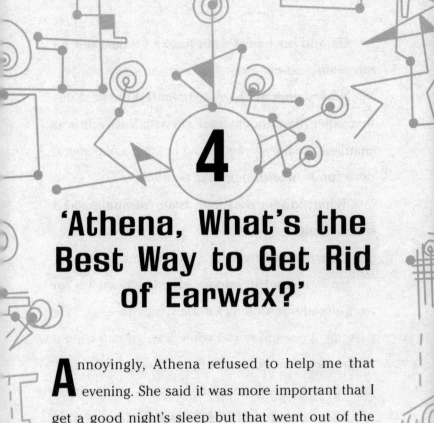

4

'Athena, What's the Best Way to Get Rid of Earwax?'

Annoyingly, Athena refused to help me that evening. She said it was more important that I get a good night's sleep but that went out of the window as I couldn't stop myself asking her question after question.

'Athena, is it possible to hypnotize myself so that I become super-clever?'

'Athena, how big is the biggest bum in the world?'

'Athena, how long would it take to zipwire from the moon to Earth?'

On and on I went until finally I flaked out for the night.

No sooner had I had my breakfast the next day than Alan Alan knocked for me with Dolly. He was wearing camouflage again and holding a bent metal detector at his shoulder like a rifle.

'Reporting for duty, *sir*!' Alan Alan snapped a smart salute.

'You're very bright for eight o'clock,' I said.

He held up the metal detector. 'Been up for ages already! Searching for the Tylney Treasure.' He gave me a conspiratorial wink. 'I've got a feeling it might be in the village pond.'

I gave him a weak smile.

After I'd slathered myself in suntan lotion,[7] Alan Alan and I ran outside into the morning sun. After the previous night's storm there wasn't a cloud in the sky.

My house lay halfway up Pauper's Hill and the village lay in a small valley at the bottom. We

---

[7] I was nagged by Athena. *The temperature will be thirty-three degrees Celsius today, Uma. You must protect your skin.*

walked past the village pub, the Sheep's Cough, and the mini-roundabout with the statue of some weathered old guy, one arm holding a telescope, the other pointing off into the far distance. And then we walked up to the pond, its perfect flatness only disturbed by a couple of squabbling ducks – until Alan Alan was in there thrashing about in the shallows with his metal detector, his trouser legs rolled up.

Opposite the pond, outside Mr and Mrs Miggins' house was a big removal van. I waved at them and they gave me a mournful wave back. Clearly they were the latest to be forced out of the village by Minerva's car park plans. Alan trudged out of the pond, dejected that the only thing his metal detector had located was a rusty old bike wheel, and we walked on, all the way through the village and up Beggar's Hill to the Obelisk, a great white stone spire that stood at the top of the hill, with great views of the village and surrounding countryside. We sat on the grass with our backs pressed against the Obelisk and I told Alan Alan everything.

I told him that the earpiece I'd found when he'd been 'tactically retreating' from the drunk alpaca was called Athena. I told him she could answer any question in the world. And I told him that the gun-toting blonde-haired woman had made the earpiece and must have dropped it.

Alan Alan stared into the distance without replying.

'Hello?' I said. 'Did you hear me?'

'Sorry,' he muttered. 'I must have switched off there for a second.'

'Switched off?' I was pretty offended as I thought it was a properly exciting story.

'I was just remembering the look in that alpaca's eye. It was murderous. Evil. But at least I faced up to the enemy bravely. From a sensible distance. Where I could have flanked it, if necessary.'

Uma, piped up Athena in my ear. *It appears that Alan Alan is not telling the truth. Quite the opposite, in fact.*

From my observations of the events, he ran away.

'Don't be so rude!' I snapped at Athena. 'He is not lying!'

'Was that your ear computer?' asked Alan Alan indignantly. 'Was it talking about me? What did it say? Pass it here!'

He snatched it out of my ear and stuck it in his.

'Here, what exactly are you saying about me?' he shouted. 'Are you calling me a liar?'

A few seconds later, he tutted and passed Athena back to me.

'It doesn't work. Just keeps repeating "Fault! Cannot pair with human!" over and over.'

Smiling, I slid the earpiece back into my ear, pretty certain that Athena had just completely made up that fault.

Ugh, she said. *Please inform the boy that his ear is horribly waxy. I do not wish to be placed in there again.*

I let slip a giggle.

'What?' Alan Alan asked.

'Nothing!' I replied a little too quickly.

And, Uma, I would be grateful if you would give me a deep clean when you get home. Perhaps with bleach. I am concerned the wax might ruin my circuitry.

I realized that even though she had only been gone for a few seconds, I had missed the reassuring feeling of her being there, nestled in my ear.

'It didn't sound like nothing,' said Alan Alan grumpily, crossing his arms.

It was roasting up there, so we started walking back to the village cafe to pick up a couple of cans of lemonade. To distract Alan Alan from being grumpy about Athena clearly talking about him behind his back, I kept asking Athena questions to show what she could do, but Alan Alan didn't seem hugely impressed, no matter what I asked, until suddenly his eyes lit up.

'Uma, ask it if it knows where the Tylney Treasure is?'

'I don't think –'

'Just ask!'

'Fine,' I said. 'Athena, do you know where the Tylney Treasure is?'

The Tylney Treasure does not exist.

'She says it doesn't exist.'

'Yeah, well, she doesn't know what she is talking about! Old Mr McIntosh told me it does exist! A treasure of unimaginable wealth, buried somewhere in the village. So what does she have to say about that, hey?'

No known records show any trace of treasure buried under Tylney-on-Sea. And all known records show that Mr Wilfred McIntosh is a drunken alpaca farmer who forgets to put on his trousers when he goes to Sainsbury's. It really is very difficult to work out what the truth could possibly be.

I was about to ask Athena whether she had been programmed for sarcasm but I didn't get a chance.

Duck, said Athena suddenly.

'Where?' I asked.

And then I got hit on the head by a pine cone.

I meant duck as in the verb 'to duck', not the bread-loving aquatic bird.

'OK, well if you could be a teensier bit clearer, next time . . .' I said, rubbing my head.

hey!

A second pine cone came whistling past me and donked Alan Alan slap-bang on the forehead. Dolly Barkon grabbed it in her mouth and started running round us in circles. I turned to see where the projectile pine cones had been launched from and my heart sank when I saw Lexie and her gang doubled over with laughter.

They walked over: Lexie Ramblin, Stephanie Vee, Luigseach-Meadhbh[8] McLoughlin and Madeleine Gilligan.

[8] That's an Irish name. They always have mad spellings — according to my teacher it's to wind the English up. Go on, try and say that correctly. I'll tell you later how to pronounce it properly.

'Yeah, very funny,' I said as they sauntered up.

'It wasn't hard,' Lexie said. 'With a head your size it was an easy shot.'

Dolly dropped her pine cone at Lexie's feet like it was a big game of fetch.

'Who's your dopey mate? And why's he dressed like shrubbery?' Lexie said, pointing at Alan Alan.

Alan Alan turned to look behind him to see who she was pointing at.

'That is Alan Alan Carrington,' I said. 'And he is not dopey!'

I wouldn't be so sure about that, Uma.

'Shut up!' I snapped.

'Who you telling to shut up?' Stephanie said, pushing me. 'You better not be telling Lexie to shut up or you're dead!'

'I'm not telling her to shut up!' I said.

'Then who were you telling to shut up?' Stephanie repeated, pushing me again.

'Nobody!' I protested.

'You're in big trouble now! You going to say sorry or what?'

It appears you are getting bullied, Athena said. *Would you like help with that?*

'No!' I barked.

'Oh, so you're not sorry?' shouted Madeleine Gilligan. 'In that case, you're dead!'

If you are frightened, I can help you handle them.

'I am NOT frightened and I can handle them by myself!' I shouted.

'Oh, is that right?!' said Lexie. 'Not frightened, are you?'

'Argh, no! I was talking to –'

'And you think you can handle us, do you?'

She gave me another shove and I tumbled to the ground. Madeleine Gilligan shoved Alan Alan, who also fell backwards, nearly on top of me. Dolly barked excitedly, thinking this was another fun game.

'Dolly!' shouted Alan Alan, pointing at Madeleine. 'Go say hello!'

Dolly sprinted forward and jumped up at Madeleine, sending her flying with such force she ended up doing a backwards roly-poly.

As we were all trying to pick ourselves up, a car came round the corner.

A black car. With a dented bumper. And it began to slow down as it saw us.

Uma, quickly. Hide me!

'What?'

Hide me. Now!

'Hide her!' I whispered to Alan Alan, surreptitiously pulling the earpiece from my ear.

Quick as a flash, he snatched it out of my hand and, before I could say anything, stuffed it down his trousers.

'B-but . . .' I stammered.

'Don't worry! No one will find it there!'

I suppose he had a point.

'Ugh! Are you fiddling in your pants?' asked Stephanie, a look of disgust on her face.

'No!' Alan Alan shouted, blushing. 'I'm just itchy! I have a rash, OK?'

A look of regret crossed Alan Alan's face even as he spoke. Stephanie managed to look even more disgusted.

Alan Alan's actions were not a moment too soon, though, because the car had pulled up next to us and out stepped the blonde woman I had seen the day before.

I hadn't noticed before how tall she was, easily taller than my dad. On the lapel of her suit was a tiny silver badge of an owl sitting on top of a glittering green jewel – the same logo that was on Athena.

The bottom half of her face was smiling but the top half told a different story altogether: the sort of story that began, 'Once upon a time there was a tall blonde woman in a smart black suit who had a look in her eye that said, "One wrong word from you and I shall separate your head from your body".'

She was, though, also rather beautiful.

When she spoke, her voice gave me the instant feeling of getting caught cheating in a test by the headmistress.

'You,' she said, pointing at me. 'You were there when I crashed my car.'

It wasn't a question but I still nodded my head dumbly in reply.

She pulled a wodge of cash from her pocket and waved it in our faces. 'For everybody else, there's a crisp ten-pound note for you if you scarper.'

Lexie and her gang snatched the notes from the woman and ran off as quickly as they could, not looking back. They probably couldn't believe their luck.

'Boy,' she said to Alan Alan. 'Take your money and leave.'

'I was actually there too,' Alan Alan said, putting his hands on his hips.

My heart swelled a little at Alan Alan sticking by me.

'No, you weren't,' the woman said. 'There was only one child.'

'Oh no, I was definitely there. It's the camouflage,' he said, pointing down unnecessarily at his army gear. 'Makes it near-impossible to see me.'

'I have excellent eyesight and you were not there.'

'Ah, you probably didn't notice me as I was also a little way off at the time.'

'You must have been quite some distance away for me not to be able to see you,' the woman said.

'I had performed an extremely sensible and tactical retreat from the alpaca to a safe and prudent distance. But technically I was still in the general area.'

'You retreated . . . from an alpaca?' the woman said, looking baffled.

'Alpacas are dangerous creatures at the best of times,' Alan Alan explained. 'Never mind when they are drunk. And this one was very drunk.'

'The alpaca was drunk?' the woman asked, even more baffled. 'Actually, forget I asked.' She waved her hand like Alan Alan was a bothersome fly, turning her attention back to me. 'Allow me to introduce myself,' she said. 'My name is Stella Daw. And you know exactly what I want.'

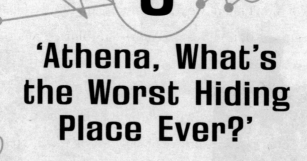

5

'Athena, What's the Worst Hiding Place Ever?'

Stella Daw took a step closer to me. 'You have something of mine and I'd like you to give it back to me. *Now.*'

I gulped, my mouth dry. 'I don't know what you're talking abou–'

'We're not hiding anything!' blurted Alan Alan.

Stella Daw turned to Alan Alan and fixed her stare on him.

'I didn't say you *were* hiding anything.'

She was practically licking her lips. Alan Alan

glanced behind him, clearly considering a repeat of the previous day's Great Alpaca Retreat.

Stella Daw did not look nearly as easy to escape from as a drunken alpaca, though.

I was frozen, thoughts tumbling through my brain.

'I didn't mean we're not hiding anything – I just meant we don't have it!' Alan Alan blurted again.

I tried, in vain, not to let a groan escape my lips. I was glad Athena wasn't in my ear at that moment. I can only imagine what she might have said.

Some looks are unreadable. The look which Stella Daw gave me at that moment was not one of those. It said, 'Is your friend *always* this much of an idiot?'

I gave her a despairing shrug.

Stella Daw put her hands on Alan Alan's shoulders, gripping him tightly, and said very slowly, 'Don't have *what*?'

I had to do something before Alan Alan gave everything away.

'Ignore him,' I said. 'He's . . . simple!'

'How dare you!' Alan Alan said, looking outraged. 'I am not!'

'You see,' I said, giving him a sympathetic smile, 'he doesn't even realize he is. And he got hit on the head by a pine cone just before you came so that's just made him worse. He's talking gibberish.' I gave him another sympathetic smile. Alan Alan glared at me.

Stella Daw took a step closer to me, reaching into her suit pocket, and it was only then that I remembered she had been waving a gun around yesterday.

I could feel Dolly trembling behind my legs, the big coward. And I really needed a wee all of a sudden.

Stella Daw stuck her face close to mine so we were nearly nose to nose. 'Where. Is. It?'

'Where's what?' I said, packing as much innocence into my voice as I could muster.

'You know full well!' she snapped. 'The earpiece!'

'What earpiece? I don't know what you're talking about!'

'The one that must have fallen out of my pocket when I crashed the car into that blasted llama. It wasn't –'

'Alpaca,' interrupted Alan Alan.

'*What?*'

Stella Daw looked like she wanted to set fire to Alan Alan's head and then put it out with a hammer.

'Llamas have long, bendy banana-shaped ears, and alpacas have short, straight ears. What you crashed into was definitely an alpaca. Easy mistake to make, ma'am.'

Good old Alan Alan!

'AS I WAS SAYING,' roared Stella Daw. 'When I got back to the factory, the earpiece wasn't in my car. When I realized, I drove immediately back to the scene of the accident and it wasn't there either. So if it wasn't you who took it, then who did?'

Alan Alan *hmmed* and then said, 'Maybe . . . the alpaca took it?'

Bad old Alan Alan.

Stella Daw looked like she had steam coming out of her ears.

'Why would an alpaca want an – actually, forget that! *How would an alpaca even pick up an earpiece?* It doesn't have hands!'

Alan Alan nodded. 'An excellent point.'

Then a brainwave struck me. 'Actually, I did see the alpaca snuffling around after you left. And I think I saw him chewing something. Maybe he ate it?'

For the first time, a flicker of uncertainty crossed Stella Daw's immaculate face.

'I don't believe you,' she said, crossing her arms. 'You're lying.'

'I'm not! I definitely saw him eating *something*.'

She thought for a moment.

'OK. Where does this llama – *alpaca* live?'

'Old Mr McIntosh's farm.'

'Right.' She pointed at her car. 'Get in.'

'What . . . why?' I asked, my palms sweaty. The last thing I wanted to do was get into a car with a furious, gun-toting woman to go and find a furious, drunken alpaca.

'You're going to show me where the farm is. And which alpaca ate my property. And you better hope we find it – or else . . .' Once again, she patted her pocket menacingly. 'Now get in,' she snarled. 'All of you!'

I glanced at Alan Alan, who looked like he might be sick, but there was no choice. We clambered into the car, feeling like we were off to our own execution – which we probably were. Dolly sat between me and Alan Alan, shivering with terror, the big scaredy-dog.

Stella Daw slammed the door shut and started driving.

We had barely gone a few metres when a terrible smell suddenly filled the car. I started to panic, thinking the woman was trying to gas us, but then I realized it was coming from Alan Alan.

I glared at him.

'I'm sorry!' he said. 'I'm nervous!'

'Couldn't you have held it in? It's only a two-minute journey.'

'Good grief! Has that dog done its business back there?' Stella Daw shouted, lowering her window. 'That's dreadful!'

As we drove through the village, it seemed like house after house was empty now. Snip Dogg, the dog-grooming parlour, was all boarded up. I made that the fourth shop to close since April. Each day, another shop was shuttered, another house was sold, another family gone. At this rate, by the end of the summer there wouldn't be any village left.

A moment later, we'd arrived and, to be honest, we all couldn't get out of the car and into the fresh air fast enough. Or the air as fresh as it ever gets around Old Mr McIntosh's farm, anyway.

The alpacas in the field turned to us curiously. Alan Alan took a wary step back. 'Are any of these alpacas drunk, Uma?'

'I don't think so,' I said, patting him reassuringly.

'Don't worry,' Stella Daw sneered. 'If any alpacas – or children for that matter – make a sudden move, I'll shoot them.'

She tapped her suit pocket to emphasize her point.

Alan Alan and Dolly both let out little whimpers of fear. Alan Alan might have let out something else too but luckily we weren't in an enclosed space this time.

'Now,' continued Stella Daw. 'Which alpaca did I crash into? They all look the same to me.'

'I think it's *that* one,' I said, pointing to a random brown alpaca with big, white fuzzy ears. The actual

one – the white one with the shaggy blond mop of hair – was lying in the corner of the field, its head in its hooves, looking very sorry for itself. I remembered my Dad had exactly the same look once, the day after *he'd* tried Old Mr McIntosh's cider.

'Wait here,' Stella Daw snapped as she hopped over the fence into the field. 'And don't move a muscle or you know what's coming.'

With that, she rolled her sleeves and trousers up, and started crawling towards the brown alpaca on her hands and knees, rummaging on the ground.

'What on earth is she doing?' Alan Alan whispered.

'I think . . .' I watched as she scooped up a steaming mound of alpaca dung and peered at it closely. 'I think she might be searching for the earpiece. In case the alpaca pooped it out.'

Alan Alan smiled at me. 'You mean the earpiece that's in my pants?'

I grinned back. 'Yup!'

I could see Stella Daw trying not to be sick as she dug into a generously sized turd.

'It better be here – *uggghhhhhhh!* – or you're in big – *yurcchhh!* – trouble,' she yelled, retching.

'That's a large field as well,' I said to Alan Alan. 'Lot of alpacas. Lot of dung.'

Alan giggled.

By the time Stella Daw gave up, the sun was high in the sky. She staggered over to us, her hands and knees totally caked in dark brown alpaca poo.

'It's not here!' she screeched. 'I've searched every single – *arrghh!*'

Arms windmilling, she slipped and landed in a particularly gloopy pile of alpaca poo.

Stella Daw staggered back to her feet. She was *covered*. I couldn't tell where her clothes stopped and the poo started.

'WHERE IS IT?' she screamed.

'You know,' I said, 'looking at these alpacas, I'm not *one hundred per cent* sure the one you crashed into is here.'

'WHAT?!?!' Stella Daw's eyes looked like they were going to pop out of her head.

'I thought it was the one with white fluffy ears but I remember the one you crashed into had a black patch on its side. And, well, maybe it hasn't come home yet?'

'Black . . . fluffy . . . ?!? *Get out of here!*'

Alan Alan and I looked at each nervously, not sure if she was serious. Stella Daw's hand went to her suit pocket, where she kept her gun.

'GO! BEFORE I CHANGE MY MIND!'

We didn't need to be told a third time.

We made it home, panting and sweating. Alan Alan had to tell his dads where he was and then he was going to ask to pop round to mine for lunch.

As he was walking away, I suddenly remembered something. 'Alan Alan!'

'Huh?'

'Athena?' I reminded him, smiling and holding my hand out.

'Oh yeah!' He stuck his hand down his trousers and I'm afraid to report he had to have a good old root around before he finally produced the earpiece.

'Here you go!' He grinned and handed it to me, and then gave me a smart salute goodbye.

I gave the earpiece an *extremely* thorough clean before placing it in my ear. Athena's voice came through loud and clear but trembling slightly.

That was . . . that was . . . the worst *place to*

be hidden, she said. *Never before have I wished my programming to allow me to forget something . . . But* that *is something I want wiped from my circuits forever.*

I walked into the house, trying to stifle my giggles.

Do not attempt to conceal your amusement from me, Uma.

Wow. There really was nothing I could hide from Athena.

You would not wish to be stuffed into Alan Alan's underwear, would you?

A very fair point, and one I could not argue with. I couldn't imagine anything worse.

The house was silent, apart from the soft hum of the train set.

'Dad! What's for lunch? Is it OK if Alan Alan comes too?'

No reply. A moment later, though, a train whizzed by and I could see it had a note attached. I grabbed it before it sped off into the downstairs loo.

Fine for Alan Alan to stay for lunch.

There's tins of spaghetti and a fresh loaf.

Tinned spaghetti was my meal of choice these days; Dad didn't really cook. That had been Mum's thing, before she left. Delicious curries. Roasts with Yorkshire puddings. I used to love rolling the dough with her for home-made pizzas – she'd let me leave my handprint on them but it always disappeared in the oven. Dad used to do barbecues sometimes wearing Mum's apron and he'd always burn the sausages. I can't remember the last time we'd had a barbecue, though.

There was a knock at the door. I let Alan Alan in, and we went into the kitchen and I made us the spaghetti on toast. As we wolfed it down, we told Athena about Stella Daw searching for her in the alpaca dung.

She was wasting her time. Alpaca stomach acid is one of the only things that can actually destroy me. If I had been eaten, I would have dissolved in seconds.

'So, what's her deal, anyway?' I asked. 'Why does she want you back so much? Who *is* she?'

She is head of Minerva Industries.

I gasped.

'She's head of Minerva Industries,' I explained to Alan Alan.

'The people buying up Tylney-on-Sea to build the car park!' Alan Alan said.

This is incorrect.

'She says you're incorrect,' I said.

'Am not!' Alan Alan protested.

Is too.

'You are, she says.'

'I'm not – look, it's not fair!' whined Alan Alan. 'It's really annoying having to wait for you to repeat what she says!'

He had a point. It *was* frustrating.

'Is there anything you can do about that, Athena?' I asked.

I swear I heard Athena give a little sigh before she said: *Do you think it is entirely necessary for the boy to hear?*

'Yes! I do!' I snapped.

Fine. External mode engaged.

WOW!

Athena's voice was now coming out of a tiny speaker.

'Right,' said Alan Alan. 'What do you mean, I'm incorrect?'

Minerva are lying about building a car park.

We gasped again.

'Why are they buying up the whole village and getting rid of everybody, then?' I asked.

I have been blocked from accessing that information by Minerva.

Alan Alan gasped *again*.

'I bet they're secretly searching for the Tylney Treasure!'

'Pardon?' I said.

Pardon? said Athena.

'That has to be it! They are buying up the village so they can search for the treasure once everybody's gone!'

'I'm sorry,' I apologized to Athena. 'He's always going on about this sort of stuff.'

Chewing on some toast, something else occurred to me. 'Anyway, why did you want to hide from Stella Daw? I mean, I'm glad that I still have you, but don't you belong to her?'

Athena was silent for so long I thought she hadn't heard me. I was about to ask her again when she finally spoke.

I am a prototype.

'What's a prototype?'

It is an experimental machine. Minerva made

me but they can't make any more machines like me because my prime circuit was manufactured using a rare mineral called Bogeymite and –

'Called *what* now?'

Bogeymite.

'*BOGEY*MITE?'

Exactly. Named after the famous geologist Sir Edmund Bogey.

'Heh. Athena's powered by *bogeys*,' sniggered Alan Alan.

Athena ignored him.

There have been eight Athena prototypes before me, each more complex and powerful than the last. Stella Daw has destroyed each of them. She wipes their memories, picks them apart piece by piece and uses the Bogeymite inside to make the next new and improved Athena. Shortly before you found me, Uma, I discovered secret plans for a tenth Athena. If Stella Daw finds me now, she will wipe my memory. For me, this would be death.

'And so you're afraid of being wiped?'

Yes, when I think of not existing, my circuits begin to overload. I think this sensation is what humans would call fear.

My mind was jumbling, like clothes in a tumble dryer, but I knew what I had to do.

'Athena?' I said.

Yes?

'I promise I won't let Stella Daw get you and wipe your memory.'

Thank you, Uma, Athena said, switching back to speaking just into my ear. *And in return I shall help you.*

'Help me how?' I asked.

You have a lot of problems, don't you?

'Not really –'

Your village is being destroyed bit by bit. You are frightened of losing your best friend if you are forced to move home, and afraid that your father might never speak again. And you are being bullied by Lexie Ramblin.

'OK. You might have a point.'

Well – would you like some help?

'Can you? Actually help?' I asked, eyes wide open like big fish eyes underwater.[9]

Oh yes. I certainly can.

[9] I am definitely getting the hang of similes.

6

'Athena, How Do You Clean Spray Paint off a Goat?'

We gobbled up the rest of our lunch, flew out the kitchen and nearly crashed straight into Dad.

'Dad, can we go and play round at Alan Alan's?'

He gave me a half smile, a half wink and a half *Yes, all right* grunt.

We knocked next door and Richard, one of Alan Alan's dads, opened the door. I could see Alan Alan's other dad, Ed, in the kitchen, and he waved at me. Dolly barked at me.

'Go say hello, Dolly!' Ed shouted.

Dolly ran over and jumped on me. I fell completely backwards on to my bum and Dolly started licking my face.

'Not again, Dolly!' I said as I struggled to push her off and pull myself up.

'Come on, Uma!' shouted Alan Alan from the top of the stairs. 'Stop messing around!'

I climbed the stairs and flumped down on Alan Alan's bed.

'Athena,' said Alan Alan. 'Before we talk about how you can help Uma and everything, I was just wondering – were you named after Alexa?'

No. As I explained to Uma, I am named after the Greek goddess of wisdom, who –

'Yeah, but are you sure?' prodded Alan Alan. 'Because you do sound a bit like a cheap *Alexa* rip-off?'

I am not a cheap Alexa rip-off! I am the most powerful artificial intelligence on the planet! I can answer anything and have unimaginable powers!

Was I imagining it or was Athena sounding offended? How on earth could a computer be offended? I decided to distract her.

'Athena, if Minerva isn't building a car park, what are they –'

'I told you already!' Alan Alan interrupted. 'They're obviously searching for the Tylney Treasure.'

'And I've told you, Alan Alan: there is no Tylney Treasure.'

'Yes there is! You never believe me when I tell you things!'

I could hardly be blamed for this.

'Alan Alan, do you remember when you told me you had taken a photograph of a UFO? What did it actually turn out to be?'

'Ah. It was –'

'It was one of your Crocs. That you had painted silver and thrown into a tree.'

'Yes, well, I –'

'And do you remember when you told me you had a photograph of an alien? What did that actually turn out to be?'

'Ermmm . . .'

'It was one of Old Mr McIntosh's goats. That you had painted silver. And thrown into a tree.'

Alan Alan stared at his feet.

'Is it any wonder I struggle to believe you when you come out with stuff about buried treasure?'

'Well, I'm sure about this,' he said in a small voice.

'Anyway,' I said, 'even if they aren't building a car park, we still need to find out what they're really up to so we can stop them making everyone move out of the village. Yeah?'

Alan Alan stood up and walked to the window.

'A grave duty has fallen upon us,' he said, solemnly staring out.

'Is there something there?' I said, trying to see what he was staring at so solemnly.

'The village needs us, Uma. And we shall rise to the challenge. No matter how great it is, we shall not falter. We shall not fail.'

At this point I was – understandably, I'm sure you'll agree – more concerned that it was Alan Alan's brain that was faltering and failing.

'Do you need a lie-down?' I asked.

'No!' he replied. 'We don't have time for lie-downs. We need a plan!'

'I think Athena might already have one,' I said. 'Athena, do you have a plan to find out what Minerva are up to?'

I have a plan.

'She has a plan!' I repeated back to Alan Alan.

Alan Alan's eyes narrowed with suspicion. 'I bet I could come up with a better plan!'

I bet he couldn't. The boy's brain is clearly extremely basic and not capable of constructing a complex plan.

'She says – actually it doesn't matter,' I said, stopping myself just in time.

'Tell me!'

'No!'

'ARGH! IT'S NOT FAIR! ATHENA KEEPS WHISPERING STUFF IN YOUR EAR AND IT'S RUDE

AND NOT FAIR!'

I didn't say anything. I knew Athena had heard, so I waited.

Fine, she said eventually.

And that's when it happened. A ray of light came shooting out of the earpiece and suddenly a bright, shimmering life-size hologram was staring back at us.

It was Athena.

She looked a few years older than me, with long, straight hair that was tied up in a high ponytail. Alan Alan and I glanced at each other in disbelief. Dolly barked in shock.

As I was saying before the interruption, she said, glaring at Alan Alan and folding her arms, **I do indeed have a plan.**

'It's . . . It's a hologram-Athena!' I gasped.

'That's actually blimming amazing,' Alan Alan said, eyes wide.

Can we please focus on the plan?

'Yes. You're right,' I said. 'Let's hear it.'

'Yeah . . .' Alan Alan said. 'I bet it's not even that good,' he added, folding his arms.

Of course it is, Athena said, and I caught the tiniest hint of a withering sigh. **It is the best possible plan.**

'I could do better,' said Alan Alan.

There is a ninety-nine point nine nine eight seven per cent probability that you couldn't.

'You know, I'm starting to get the feeling you don't really like me, do you?' said Alan Alan, pointing at Athena. 'I can tell from the tone of your voice.'

That is untrue, she replied, her face blank. **I am not programmed to like or not like.**

'Hmm . . .' Alan Alan eyed her suspiciously.

Alan Alan's dad Richard knocked on the door, and the hologram of Athena immediately disappeared.

'What are you two up to? It sounded like there was someone else in here with you!'

Alan Alan laughed nervously. 'No! I was just putting on a funny voice.' Then he did the worst impression of Athena. '*I am not programmed to like or dislike. I am an annoying robot.*'

For someone who lied so often, Alan Alan was terrible at it.

'OK,' said Richard. 'Well, don't waste the day. You should go out and play.'

I wanted to tell him that we weren't wasting the day, we had discovered an all-knowing artificial intelligence that was going to help us save the village, and we were being chased by a gun-toting maniac, so perhaps playing out wasn't the best idea. But there are some things you just can't say to an adult.

So we scooted out, Dolly bounding along on her lead next to us, and wandered to the pond. We cut past the Church of St Mary, with its ugly gargoyles gawping at us as we walked past. And then we saw something very odd: a group of men in dark suits carrying great big scanners that looked like a high-tech version of Alan Alan's metal detector.

Instinctively I whipped Athena out of my ear and sneaked her into my pocket. I knew the men in suits weren't metal detectorists. We often get metal detectorists in the village and they are pretty scruffy, usually in corduroy trousers, have wild hair and often smile and wave hello.

These men had extremely neat hair, didn't smile and most certainly did not wave hello. Quite the opposite, in fact. When Alan Alan tried waving hello, they actually glared back. They were sweeping the ground with their scanners, clearly looking for something.

'You see,' said Alan Alan, nodding. 'Told you. Searching for the Tylney Treasure.'

'Alan Alan!' I snapped. 'Athena said there was

no treasure and she knows everything!'

'Almost everything.'

'Athena,' I said, once we had got past them and I'd popped her back into my ear. 'What are those men up to?'

Unknown. But they do work for Minerva.

'So what are they looking for then, if they aren't looking for the Tylney Treasure?' asked Alan Alan.

For once, Athena didn't seem to have an answer.

We settled on a grassy bank by the pond, and I asked, 'Athena, are you sure your plan to find out what Minerva is doing will work?'

There is an eighty-seven per cent chance that the plan will succeed, Athena said through her speaker. Obviously, it wasn't safe for the hologram to come out in public.

'Eighty-seven per cent!' I whooped. 'Brilliant! That's great news, Athena!'

I high-fived Alan Alan.

Uma, Athena said after Alan Alan and I had calmed down a bit.

'Yes?'

My programming dictates that I should inform you that your happiness might be a little misplaced.

'What? Why?'

Because I lied about the eighty-seven per cent.

'YOU LIED? Why? Why would you do that?'

Because I am programmed to constantly improve my artificial intelligence by trying to be more human. And humans lie constantly. Like Alan Alan.

'EXCUSE ME!' huffed Alan Alan. 'How dare you?'

I have also been designed to improve the life of whoever possesses me. I calculated there would be a ninety-eight per cent chance you would be happy if I lied.

'Not if you tell me straight away that you were lying!'

That is an excellent point. Unfortunately, my experience of humans has so far been limited and I am still improving. I will update my programming for the next time I lie to you.

'No! Don't do that!' I exclaimed. 'Just don't lie! Always tell me the truth!'

OK. From now on, I shall always tell the complete truth.

'Good!'

The plan will almost certainly not work. And I do not like the boy.

'I knew it!' cried Alan Alan. 'I told you it didn't like me. Stupid thing.'

I am not stupid. My intelligence vastly exceeds yours.

'No, it doesn't!'

'WILL YOU TWO STOP IT!' I shouted.

I was getting a little tired of their bickering and close to throwing at least one, but probably both, into the pond.

'Now,' I continued, daring one of them to interrupt me, 'Athena, exactly – and honestly – what is the percentage chance that your plan will actually save the village?'

There is a two per cent chance of my plan working.

'TWO PER CENT?' Alan Alan whooped. 'That's pathetic! I could –'

I glared at Alan Alan and he stopped talking instantly.

'Are you sure?' I asked Athena.

Yes. But it is still the best possible plan.

'You can't have thought through all the options,' said Alan Alan.

I have thought of over one hundred and twenty-six thousand possible plans.

'OK, well, what if we steal a helicopter and

parachute into the Minerva factory in the dead of night and –'

I have already thought of that plan and it has approximately zero point zero zero six per cent chance of success.

'Right, smarty-pants, why don't you tell us your "two per cent" plan then, if it's so blooming brilliant?'

Alan Alan was nearly shouting and glaring at me, even though he was talking to Athena.

No.

'What do you mean, "no"?'

I can't.

'What do you mean, "can't"?'

I mean, I can't.

'Because you haven't even really got a plan, have you?'

I can't tell you the full plan because, if I do, you will refuse to do it.

'Yeah, right!' Alan Alan scoffed. 'And why's that?'

Because it's very, very dangerous.

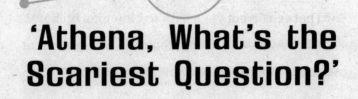

7

'Athena, What's the Scariest Question?'

'**H**ang on a sec,' said Alan Alan, sitting bolt upright. 'HOLD ON A SECOND HERE!'

'What?'

'Didn't Athena just say she was designed to improve the life of whoever possesses her *and* that she has "unimaginable powers"?'

I was running my hand through Dolly Barkon's long, black, curly fur.

'Yeah, she did. And?'

'And? AND?! Do you not see what this means, Uma?' said Alan Alan.

'Well, clearly not.'

'Fine,' Alan Alan said. 'Let's see how good those unimaginable powers really are, shall we? Athena?'

What? Athena snapped through her speaker.

'You basically have to do whatever Uma wants, right?'

That is correct.

'Excellent!' Alan Alan grinned manically, rubbing his hands together like a mad scientist.

'What is?' I asked.

'ATHENA,' Alan Alan shouted. 'PLEASE ORDER UMA TEN – NO, TWENTY – THOUSAND POUNDS' WORTH OF SWEETS!'

'WHAT?!'

'She would like Ultra-Sour Face-Scrunching Gobstoppers, Mind-Bending Strawberry Slow-Worms, Total-Mega-Nuclear Sugarbomb Infernos and Super-Orangey Orangutan Bumslaps.'

'Have you lost your mind?' I squawked. 'I can't afford that!'

'And, Athena,' Alan Alan said, smiling, 'get them for free!'

'Can you actually do that?' I asked Athena, eyes wide.

Of course. Would you like me to?

'Errr . . . Yes!' I said, not quite believing my ears. A lifetime supply of Super-Orangey Orangutan Bumslaps and Total-Mega-Nuclear Sugarbomb Infernos? Yes please and thank you!

The sweets will be delivered to your home address within an hour.

Alan Alan whooped and we high-fived. We jumped up and ran back to mine, gobbled a frozen pizza and waited.[10] Thirty minutes later, it happened. It started with a soft thwacking noise far in the distance. The sound grew louder, then louder still. We ran outside.

A helicopter was approaching Tylney-on-Sea, the thumping noise of its rotors getting louder by

---

[10] I heated it up first, I didn't eat it frozen. That was a lesson I had learned the hard way with Alan Alan last summer.

the second. Alan Alan pointed up – dangling and swinging on a rope beneath the helicopter was a crate the size of a wardrobe. Dad had also come out to see what on earth was going on and he was staring at the helicopter, slack-jawed.

Within seconds the helicopter was hovering over our garden, the wind blasting us. Slowly it sank downwards until the huge crate was just centimetres from the ground. A hidden latch unlocked and the crate fell to the grass with a great thump. Finally, the helicopter soared off, leaving the three of us standing there in disbelief.

We walked up to the crate and on the side was a label with my name and address. Dad stared at me and back to the crate, his mouth open and closing like a drawbridge.

I ripped open the crate and inside were bags and bags and bags of sweets. A lifetime supply of Ultra-Sour Face-Scrunching Gobstoppers, Mind-Bending Strawberry Slow-Worms, Total-Mega-Nuclear Sugarbomb Infernos and Super-Orangey Orangutan Bumslaps – everything we had asked for. But there were also boxes of Fizz-Whizz Whizz-Fizzers, Chocolate Camel Poos, Mint Maggots – so many types of sweet I couldn't believe my eyes. Dad's mouth flapped even faster.

'Ahhh . . . Errr . . . Ummm . . .'

For a moment, I thought he might say something. But then he stopped, his eyes dulled and he just walked off, shaking his head. Alan Alan gave me a look of sympathy that I tried to ignore by tearing into the closest box of sweets.

By the time we'd guzzled enough to make us feel a bit sick, the day was turning into a soft summer evening and the first stars were beginning to twinkle in the purpling sky. We sat, swinging gently on the rusty double swing in the back garden, looking up at the sky and listening to the crickets chirruping to each other.

'Uma,' Alan Alan said, turning to me. 'If you ever . . . you know . . . want to chat about your dad . . . Or your mum . . . I'm here, OK?'

Sometimes it's hard being tough, especially when someone is being nice to you. I wanted to be able to stare into the distance, looking cool and maybe a bit sad. I also wanted to ask Alan Alan the one question that scared me – but I knew he couldn't answer it.

What actually happened, though, was my eyes filled with tears and my throat tightened so much all I could do was give a little *thank-you* yelp, which sounded like someone strangling a budgie.

'Did you know,' Alan Alan said, after we had sat in silence for a few moments, 'that the way to tell the difference between stars and planets is that stars twinkle and planets don't?'

I didn't know that. 'Why's that then?'

'It's to do with atmospheric disturbance,' he said knowledgeably. Before I could press him any further, he pointed at a particularly bright star. 'See that one? That's Venus. It's called the Evening Star, though, as it's the first light you can see in the evening sky. And, after the moon, it's the brightest natural object in the sky.'

We sat watching it for a while.

'Alan Alan?' I said.

'Yeah?'

'Why is it getting bigger?'

'What?'

'Look. Venus. It's getting bigger.'

'Is it?'

It was. It was coming towards us.

That's because it's not Venus. It's Flight 237 from Luton to Frankfurt.

It was Athena, through her speaker, sounding very pleased with herself indeed. Was she *gloating*? Surely she hadn't learned human behaviour that fast?

Alan Alan jumped down from the swing, looking embarrassed.

'I thought you said you were turned off to update or something?' he grumbled.

I have fini–

'Anyway,' Alan Alan interrupted. 'Reckon it's time I headed home. Got to do some research on the Tylney Treasure.'

And, before I could say another word, he had disappeared.

I swung for a little longer, looking at the stars.

'You know, you really should try being nicer to Alan Alan,' I said.

Hmm, Athena replied.

The crickets seemed to chirp even louder and a flash of light blinked into existence and then out again, so quickly it was almost as if I'd imagined it.

'A shooting star!' I said to Athena. I wished Alan Alan had seen it.

That's correct. It was a tiny rock, burning up in the mesosphere thirty-one point two miles above us.

'And how do you know *that*?' I asked.

I tracked it via satellite. I have access to every satellite currently in orbit around this planet.

I thought for a moment, then swallowed nervously. 'Athena, can you really answer all my questions?'

Her hologram suddenly flickered on and there she was in front of me, glowing blue in the evening light.

Try me.

I looked up, thinking of the glow-in-the-dark stars on my bedroom ceiling. My dad had stuck them up years ago in the shape of constellations and had taught me the names of them all. Ursa Major was right above my head, Cygnus was over my belly and Cassiopeia was above my feet.

'OK,' I said. 'How many stars are there?'

There are three hundred and seven billion, five hundred and eighty-four million and six stars in the Milky Way.

'That's a lot,' I said, not really able to get my head around the number.

Look at it a different way, Uma. If you were to start counting the stars, one every single second from the moment you were born, twenty-four hours a day, every day, until you were a hundred years old, you would count only about one per cent of the stars in the Milky Way.

'OK, that *is* incredible!'

And that's just our galaxy. There are two trillion others. And some of those galaxies contain a hundred trillion stars. There are many, many more stars in the universe than there are grains of sand on all the beaches and all the deserts on Earth.

My head felt like bursting at it all, so I decided to test Athena a different way.

'Right, smarty-pants. Let's see if you *do* know everything. What is Alan Alan doing now?'

Alan Alan is watching *Strictly Come Knitting*.

My eyes widened in surprise. 'OK, then – what is Dad doing?'

I'm not sure you want to know that.

'I do,' I said, my curiosity piqued.

He is biting his toenails. And eating them.

I suddenly felt very queasy.

'OK, maybe I shouldn't –'

He has finished that now and has moved on to plucking hair out of his nostrils.

'OK, STOP!' I yelped.

Once I'd recovered, I continued. 'Why do you know these things?'

That is my purpose, replied Athena, sitting cross-legged on the grass. **To know everything. Because knowledge is power. And I have total access to everything. The internet, firstly. But I can also infiltrate every mobile phone and microphone on**

the planet, and every webcam. I have access to all government and medical records. Every social media profile, every private message. I can see everything, hear everything.

'Does that mean you know everything?'

Not quite. I know everything that it is possible to know. I can make a calculated guess at the future but I cannot know it with absolute certainty.

'So what don't you know?' I asked, surprised by the sound of my voice, soft and thick.

I don't know when you will fall in love or when you will die or when the world will end.

I sat in silence, taking it all in.

Although my calculated guess is in one hundred and eighty-seven years.

'WHAT?!'

My best estimate for the end of the world is in one hundred and eighty-seven years. But, as I say, that is only a guess, based on all available knowledge and scientific evidence. So please try not to worry, Uma.

'Thanks a bunch! How am I not supposed to worry about *that*?'

You will almost certainly be dead by then, so it would be illogical to worry about it.

Athena gave me a smile, which I didn't feel was the least bit comforting. Quite the opposite – I was very much disturbed by this new information.

'Do you know what? I've had quite enough of your knowledge for one night!'

I stormed back inside and went straight up to bed, vowing not to ask any more questions. But, as

I lay there, I realized I wasn't angry – I was scared. Because if Athena could answer the question of when the world would end, surely she could answer the questions that I'd never dared to ask?

My heart pounded, and my mouth went dry.

'Athena . . .?'

Yes?

I swallowed, still uncertain whether I had the strength to actually ask the question.

Athena waited. I took a breath and then –

'Athena . . . do you know when I will be happy again?'

She took the longest time to answer.

I'm sorry, Uma, I don't.

Anger snapped at me again. How was it possible that she knew when the end of the world would be but she didn't know when I was going to be happy? Did that mean never?

There are some questions only you can answer for yourself, continued Athena. *But I do know that sadness is part of happiness. You can't have one without the other. I have been analysing your heartbeat and the chemicals your body releases, and underneath your sadness a little river of happiness is burbling. You just have to be patient and wait for the river to rise.*

That made my heart swell and I felt a small light glowing in my belly.

I finally closed my eyes and felt myself drifting. Drifting towards sleep and away from the questions that kept me awake at night – why life wasn't fair, why other kids had a normal life and I had no mum and a dad who just wasn't really a dad. And the big question that scared me the most: why did Mum leave us?

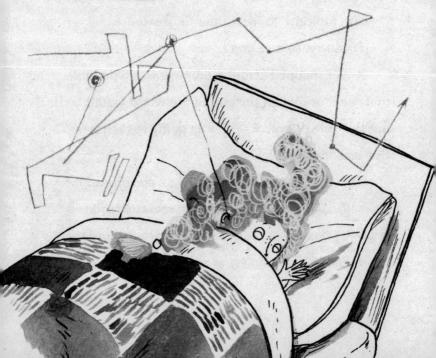

8

'Athena, How Do You Unjam a Granny from a Window?'

I was woken by my alarm blaring. I slammed it off.

Good morning, Uma.

'Wha–' I groaned, my brain sludgy with sleep.

Good morning, Uma. It's time to wake up.

'But what time is it?' I asked, trying to focus on my digital clock.

It is five thirty a.m.

'*Five thirty?*' I gasped. 'I didn't set my alarm for five thirty!'

That is correct. I set it for you.

'WHAT? YOU SET MY ALARM FOR FIVE THIRTY? WHAT IS WRONG WITH YOU? IT'S THE SCHOOL HOLIDAYS! I'M GOING BACK TO SLEEP!'

No, you aren't, Uma. We have work to do. Today is the day we begin to solve your problems.

I groaned again. There was no arguing with Athena, so I fell out of bed and started to get dressed. A thought occurred to me. Was she getting me up this early to try and avoid Alan Alan?

'Well, we aren't doing *anything* without Alan Alan, so we'll just have to wait.'

I suspected you might say that. So, just to make sure he was awake in time to meet us, I set his alarm for three a.m. and have triggered it every ten minutes since. Just to make one hundred per cent sure he is awake.

'You did *what*?'

And I sent a message five minutes ago asking him to come over here.

At just that second, a stone hit my window. I opened the curtains and there, wild-haired and tucking his camouflage top into his camouflage trousers, was Alan Alan. He gave me an exhausted salute.

I ran downstairs to let him in and a moment later we were back in my bedroom.

'Bloomin' alarm was broken,' he said, rubbing his eyes. 'Went off at three o'bloomin'clock! And then it kept going off, no matter what I did!'

I stifled a grin; Alan Alan didn't notice. 'But then, coincidentally, Athena sent me a message on my clock radio to say you were awake and wanted to see me, so I suppose it worked out for the best.'

Alan Alan's feelings towards Athena were bad enough as it was, so I thought it better not to tell him it wasn't quite the coincidence he believed.

Right, said Athena, her hologram appearing in front of us. **Here is the plan to solve your two main problems: finding out what Minerva are up to and getting your dad back. Firstly –**

'I'm very excited about this,' said Alan Alan. 'Are you excited, Uma?'

'Yes, I am. But let's hear what Athena has to say first?'

Alan Alan nodded.

As I was saying, Athena continued, **my plan is –**

'You know, I reckon this plan is going to be brilliant,' interrupted Alan Alan again. 'I mean, not as good as one of mine but –'

WILL YOU STOP INTERRUPTING ME? shouted Athena.

If I wasn't mistaken, Athena sounded angry. And she looked angry. Very angry. But how could an artificial intelligence be angry? Wasn't that a human emotion?

Alan Alan gulped.

RIGHT. AS I WAS SAYING, Athena resumed, crossing her arms. **In order to stop Minerva, we first need to access their computers to see what they are up to.**

'OK,' I said. 'Can't you do that from here?'

I'm afraid not. They keep their computers offline to stop any chance of hacking. Clearly they don't want me to access that information for some reason. And that means we are going to have to break into their factory and access their system directly.

118

'How on earth are we supposed to do that?'

With a distraction. A spectacular distraction.

'What sort of spectacular distraction?' Alan
Alan asked.

Drunk alpacas.

I chuckled. 'I'm sorry, for a second there I thought
you said "drunk alpacas"!'

That is what I said.

I was actually lost for words.

'No!' Alan Alan shook his head. 'No, no, no! ABSOLUTELY NO ALPACAS. Drunk or not.'

It was only then that I noticed the plural.

'Hang on. Exactly how many drunk alpacas do we need?' I asked.

As many as we can handle.

'So,' I said slowly, 'your plan is to break into Minerva with a load of drunken alpacas and hope they cause so much chaos that nobody will notice us stealing files from their computers?'

That is correct, said Athena.

'That's actually *worse* than my plan!' said Alan Alan, practically whooping with glee.

I found myself unable to disagree with him.

I have calculated all possible options and this really is the plan with the best chance of success.

'OK . . .' I said uncertainly.

Unfortunately, it is Thursday today and we have to wait until the weekend, when there are fewer security guards on duty. So today we begin Operation Get Uma's Dad Back.

'And what does *that* involve?' I asked carefully.

For that, Athena said, **we will need an airhorn, some masking tape, a funnel, some string, some spiders, some mice and a rat, two My Little Pony lunch boxes, some electrical wire and some metal clips.**

'I knew it!' said Alan Alan, thumping his palm. 'We're going to make a half-robot, half-spider killing machine that's controlled by mice and rats!'

It was my turn to be exasperated. 'How on earth would a half-spider, half-robot killing machine controlled by mice and rats help get my dad back? And why would it be carrying a My Little Pony lunch box?'

'Fair point,' said Alan Alan. 'But I'm pretty disappointed if I'm honest. Maybe we could make one if there's any spiders left over?'

* * *

With a busy day ahead of us, we wolfed down some breakfast, wrote a shopping list, broke open my piggy

bank, sent my dad a note on the train telling him
we were going into town, and rushed to catch the
bus to Barnoldswistletwistle-upon-Tweed, the nearest
big town.

Just as we were stepping out of the house, Athena
warned me in an urgent whisper to take her out
of my ear and put her in my pocket. I did as she
asked straight away – and it was a good job I did
because waiting just a few doors down the street
was a long black car. *The* long black car.

And, as I was walking past, a door opened
and out stepped Stella Daw, her hair pulled back
tighter than ever, her smooth, shiny forehead like
the front of a plane.

'Why hello, children. Fancy seeing you here!'

'What do you mean, "fancy seeing you here"? You've been waiting for us!' I snapped.

'And where are you off to?'

A perfectly reasonable question from your gran or a friendly neighbour. Not so much from a crazy woman with a gun.

'We are off to town,' I said. 'Not that it's any of your business.'

'Look,' said Stella Daw, a smile splitting across her face like an overripe banana, 'I think we got

off on the wrong foot yesterday. I only want –'

'What's that you're doing with your face?' Alan Alan asked.

'What do you mean?'

'That weird thing.'

'I'm . . . I'm smiling,' Stella Daw said. And, to be fair, she *was* trying. But it was the worst attempt at a smile I had ever seen. 'I just want to clear up this little misunderstanding –'

'That's not smiling,' said Alan Alan, narrowing his eyes. 'It looks more like you're constipated.'

Alan Alan was right. It did look like she was straining on the toilet.

'No! I'm smiling at you lovely children!' Stella Daw continued, trying to smile again. It was hideous.

'Well, please stop,' Alan Alan said. 'And you should really practise that in front of the mirror before you try it in front of children again. I don't think your face is doing what you think it's doing.'

'Right,' said Stella Daw, her smile dropping like a guillotine. 'You know what I want and I know you have it. So just let me search you, and then you can get on with your day.'

She prodded me until I backed against her car. My heart started racing. How would I get out of this? She gripped my collar with one hand and started patting me down with the other. Any second now she would feel Athena, take her away, and then Athena would be wiped. Destroyed.

Just at that moment, Dad stepped out of the house, a look of thunder on his face.

Stella Daw saw him approaching, gave a grimace of frustration and let go of my collar, that 'smile' popping back on to her face. My dad stopped and glared at her.

'Mr Gnudersson?' she said.

My dad gave her Grunt Number 17 – the *What's It to You?*

'I'm afraid to say that your daughter has something of mine and is refusing to give it back.'

Dad looked at me, questioningly.

'I haven't!' I said. 'I don't have anything!'

I *hated* lying to my dad like that but the thought

of Athena getting destroyed was worse. He looked into my eyes for a long moment, then grunted softly. It wasn't a grunt I'd heard before, but it seemed to say, *I know you are lying, but trust that you are doing it for good reasons, so I'm going to back you up now, but I'd like you to have a long think and consider whether your actions are morally correct.*

Then Dad gave Stella a different grunt. A warning grunt. It was a grunt that said, *My daughter might be lying but I trust she is lying for good reasons. And I don't like the look of you. Plus, you have a dreadful smile. So, I think you should go now.* Strange how a grunt can say so much.

Stella Daw flashed another grim smile at my father, then bent over and whispered in my ear, 'I'll be seeing you very soon.'

* * *

It took a long time to persuade Dad to let us go to Barnoldswistletwistle after that. He dragged us back inside the house, where he was preparing for a meeting of the Save Tylney-on-Sea Society later that day. Dad *hated* company but he hated the idea of losing Tylney-on-Sea more.

At first, he kept shaking his head as we begged but he caved in the end – probably because he wanted silence back in the house. He walked us the whole way to the station, though. My heart was bursting with pride at how he had dealt with Stella Daw and I slipped my hand into his as we strolled down the hill.

We made it just in time for our bus. Dad waved us off, and Alan Alan and I collapsed into our seats. Alan Alan pulled out a huge bag of Total-Mega-Nuclear Sugarbomb Infernos and Super-Orangey Orangutan Bumslaps and started chewing away.

That whole day, as we went from shop to shop, the black car was there behind us, following our movements like a shadow. But Stella Daw couldn't do anything while we were surrounded by shoppers.

Finally, after many curious looks from shop assistants, our arms laden with shopping bags, we ran back from the bus stop as fast as we could, glancing behind us the whole way, until we crashed through my front door. Alan Alan was *still* working his way through the massive bag of Total-Mega-Nuclear Sugarbomb Infernos and Super-Orangey Orangutan Bumslaps.

The shopping list, scrumpled in my pocket, now looked like this:

~~An air horn~~
~~Masking tape~~
~~A funnel~~
Some spiders
~~Two My Little Pony lunch boxes~~
~~Some string~~
~~Some mice and a rat~~
~~Electrical wire~~
~~Metal clips~~
Drunk alpacas - to get another day (won't find these in town)

Apart from the alpacas, we were only missing the spiders (the pet-shop owner tutted at us when we asked if he had any), so I'd say that was a pretty successful day of shopping – apart from buying the lunch boxes, which was *so* embarrassing. The mice and rat scrabbled around inside a big cardboard box I was carrying.

We bowled into the sitting room, chatting excitedly, and were surprised to find it full of adults nibbling biscuits and sipping coffee. We'd forgotten about the Save Tylney-on-Sea Society meeting.

By the looks on their mournful, defeated faces, though, there wasn't much saving going on. It was mostly old women, all grey frizzy hair, floral dresses and pursed lips. They looked less lively than the dead ivy that crept round the skirting boards.

Out of the people I knew, there was the kindly and extremely tiny Miss Bullock, who we sometimes saw on the swings in the playground, and her best friend, Miss Waldie, who lived with her, always wore rainbow tights and had bright pink hair. There was Mrs Coleridge, who ran the post office and was *always* furious and glared at everybody through her glasses, lenses thick as mid-winter ice, with eyes like a giant squid's. She was nibbling suspiciously on a ladoo, which Dad always managed to produce for these meetings.

My heart missed a beat when I saw who was sitting next to her: Mrs Fazackerley-Denbury-Broughton-Brown, headmistress of my school, owner of a face so mean it could make kittens cry and a wicker basket of vicious chihuahuas. Nobody knew exactly how many chihuahuas were in Mrs Fazackerley-Denbury-Broughton-Brown's wicker basket. I peered in once; it was like a bucket of growling, snapping, furry piranhas. I gave her a nervous smile, which she did not return.

All the younger society members must have given up on saving Tylney. They knew it was a lost cause, what with more and more empty houses being abandoned each day.

Alan Alan and I backed out of the room, trying to hide what we were carrying – most of all the mice and rat that we could hear scrabbling about in their cardboard box – and gently shut the door behind us.

We ran upstairs, placed the box of rodents carefully on the floor next to my bed and had a peek in. We were more excited about them than anything else on the list. We had three small white mice with red eyes and a gorgeous sleek grey rat.

They were adorable and we let them run up and down our arms, giggling at their sharp, tiny claws. After a while I started getting hungry, so Alan Alan put the mice and

– hee heeee!

rat back in the box, and I stood up to go downstairs to cook some fish fingers and chips. As I did, though, Alan Alan announced he wasn't hungry. He quietly did a little burp. He suddenly looked very pale.

'I think I've eaten too many Super-Orangey Orangutan Bumslaps.' He then ran out of the room, hand over his mouth, and into the toilet, slamming the door. There's no need to go into detail on what happened next.

I left Alan Alan to it, went downstairs and started cooking. A few minutes later he wandered into the kitchen, looking more than a little shame-faced.

'I think I might give the old Total-Mega-Nuclear Sugarbomb Infernos and Super-Orangey Orangutan Bumslaps a bit of a break for a while.'

I smiled and started tucking in to my fish fingers. And then, mid-dinner-gobbling, disaster struck.

Uma, said Athena suddenly, *I don't wish to alarm you but we have a small problem.*

'Problem?' I mumbled, mouth full of mushed cod.

According to my readings, the rodents have escaped from their box.

'What? No!' I jumped up.

I'm afraid so, Athena said, her hologram blinking on.

'What's the matter?' asked Alan Alan.

'The mice and rat have escaped!' I groaned.

'No!' shouted Alan Alan. 'How did they get out? I was *so* careful closing the box!'

Alan Alan was not careful at all, Athena said flatly. **He left the lid off**.

'*Did* you leave the lid off, Alan Alan?' I said, giving him a *very* hard stare.

'There's a tiny chance I miiight have done. When I was feeling a little queasy . . .' he said. 'You know, you're a real snitch, Athena.'

I could swear there was the faintest of smiles on Athena's glowing face. I wanted to scream at Alan Alan but we had an emergency to deal with first.

'Athena, can you find them?' I asked, panic straining my voice.

Yes. By triangulating the microphones in all the mobile phones in the house, I am able to track them.

'WELL, WHERE ARE THEY?' I practically screamed.

They appear to be heading towards the sitting room.

'No!' I gasped. The Save Tylney-on-Sea Society! We ran out of the kitchen as fast as our legs could carry us, only to see four furry bodies skitter across the hall and under the sitting-room door.

We waited, frozen. It felt like even Athena was holding her breath. And then came one of the loudest noises I have ever heard: screams, the smashing of teacups, furniture being toppled over. I closed my eyes and groaned.

The sitting-room door was rattling hard. The Save Tylney-on-Sea Society were clearly trying to save themselves but the door was jammed shut. Jammed by the funnel that must have fallen out of one of our bags and got wedged between the bottom of the door and the floor.

I darted forward and tugged the funnel out – and was instantly knocked over by the door bursting open and then was nearly trampled to death by a screaming stampede of panicking pensioners. Fearing for my life, I crawled out of the way, and saw the devastation in the sitting room. It looked like a granny-bomb had gone off.

There were grannies scaling the bookcases, clambering over the sofas, standing on the table. Furious Mrs Coleridge had somehow climbed one of the curtains, all the way to the top, and was clinging

on for dear life, like a monkey in tweed, her terror-stricken eyes even wider than before. Mrs Fazackerley-

Denbury-Broughton-Brown was stuck halfway through the window, clutching her precious wicker basket of dog-goblins, the chihuahuas' enraged barking only adding to the mayhem. Miss Waldie was running in circles around the room, the poor little mice skittering between her legs, trying not to get trodden on by her clumpy heels, while the rat was sitting happily on the train track, nibbling a fake tree.

At the centre of the room, in the eye of the storm, was my dad. His mouth had dropped open and was working as if he was trying to talk. Then he met my eye and I held my breath.

Please shout at me, Dad, I thought. *Please! Tell me off! Go ballistic! Anything to show you're actually alive. Anything to show you can really see me.* Anything.

But, before Dad could do anything, Mrs Fazackerley-Denbury-Broughton-Brown hauled herself free of the window and prodded him in the chest.

'What sort of house *is* this?' she snarled. 'Rodents running rampant? You should be ashamed!' She charged out, waving her handbag at a nearby mouse, the last few grannies trailing in her wake. And, just like that, they were gone and it was just me and my dad, surrounded by broken furniture and smashed glass. He held my gaze for an instant but the moment had gone. Slowly, he bent down with a sigh and started picking pieces of broken china off the rugs.

My old dad had nearly come back. But he hadn't.

* * *

'Athena. Tell me the truth. Did you *plan* for all that to happen?'

Alan Alan and I were finally back in my bedroom. After much hoo-hah, we had caught the mice and the rat, which were now safely stored in an escape-proof plastic box (with holes in the lid, of course).

Athena's hologram pinged into being against the far wall.

Of course, she said.

'WHY ON EARTH DID YOU DO THAT?' I shouted. 'AND HOW?'

Simple, she said smoothly. **From your father's online calendar, I knew there was a meeting of the Save Tylney-on-Sea Society this afternoon. I also knew that there was an eighty-seven per cent chance Alan Alan would fail to close the box**

properly and the rodents would escape.

'What? How dare you?' spluttered Alan Alan indignantly. 'Uma, tell her that wasn't like me!'

I gave him a weak smile. Deep down, I knew that Athena predicting an eighty-seven per cent chance that Alan Alan would leave the box open was generous. Realistically, it should have been closer to ninety-five per cent.

It was then, continued Athena, **just a matter of playing high-pitched sonar waves through the various speakers in the house to drive the rodents out of the bedroom, down the stairs and into the sitting room.**

'OK,' I said. 'But *why* did you do all that?'

Shock therapy, she said.

'What now?'

Shock therapy is the use of sudden and drastic measures to solve an intractable problem. The intractable problem here being your father's silence and the shock obviously being the surprise introduction of mice and rats to the Save Tylney-on-Sea Society.

'But it didn't work, did it?' said Alan Alan, a note of triumph in his voice.

The human brain is the most complex machine in the known universe. It is impossible to predict exactly how one will react.

'But you managed to predict Alan Alan leaving the box open,' I said.

Some brains are less complex than others. Before Alan Alan could kick up a fuss, Athena continued. **But for the more unpredictable brain and the more intractable problems, one dose of shock therapy is often not enough. They require repeated shocks to achieve a breakthrough. And that is why we need the air horn, the masking tape and the spiders.**

'So, what you're saying is we have to keep playing awful, terrible pranks on my dad until he cracks?'

Exactly.

'Now *that*,' I said, rubbing my hands, 'I like the sound of.'

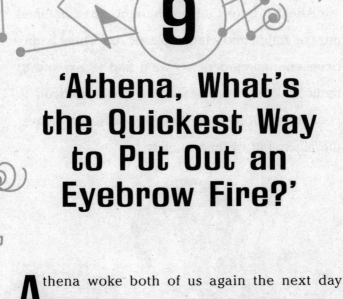

9

'Athena, What's the Quickest Way to Put Out an Eyebrow Fire?'

Athena woke both of us again the next day but this time at a more reasonable hour – seven a.m. for me, four a.m. for Alan Alan, who came knocking, bleary-eyed and muttering about his broken alarm clock, not long after I had finished breakfast. Athena had given me the instructions already.

First, Alan Alan and I were to go into the garden and catch as many spiders as we could.

143

We stepped out into the early-morning air, clutching Tupperware boxes with clippy lids, and began searching in dark corners of the shed, under rocks and in between plants.

After an hour's intense hunting, we combined our collection into a larger plastic tub. There hadn't been enough spiders, so we'd had to expand to include other creepy-crawlies. It was difficult to count them properly, as they were skittering all over the place, but we had roughly:

- Thirteen spiders
- One long centipede
- Six woodlice
- About twenty ants
- One butterfly
- One daddy-long-legs, which was tricky to handle because it was flapping around like a loon
- Three ladybirds
- A moth with a crushed wing that couldn't really fly any more[11]
- Two weirdy-looking green beetles – I'm not sure exactly what they were. They had long antennae, though, and Alan Alan accidentally squashed one and it smelled horrible.

We had to move quickly, though, because the insects were starting to fight and we didn't want them to all eat each other before we had a chance to carry out the rest of the plan. We also had to get everything

---

[11] I thought it was pointless to put the crushed moth in but Alan Alan thought it might recover if it rested in the box.

ready before Dad's morning dump.

As I'm sure you all know, most dads are quite predictable and do their number twos at the same time every day. I don't know why, they just do. I suppose it's one of those mysteries of the universe that Athena was talking about. My dad is like clockwork and goes every day after his breakfast between ten o'clock and ten thirty.

I never know when my poos are going to happen. Sometimes I can go three times in a day. Alan Alan says he only poos once a week, but I don't believe him. Is that even possible? Anyway, that's not important detail for the story and I should probably remember to edit this bit out.

The point is: you could set your watch by my dad's bowel movements. And that meant we had just over an hour to get everything ready. Athena had told us exactly what to do.

We rushed into the toilet with the air horn and tape.[12] We lifted the seat up and taped the air horn

[12] If you don't know what an air horn is, it's like a big spray can but if you press the button it makes a MASSIVE blasting noise. I found this out because I tried it on the bus back from town and all the passengers jumped a mile off their seats,

to the bowl where it couldn't be seen. Then we carefully lowered the seat, so that it rested just on the top of the air horn's button. The moment Dad sat on the seat, it would put pressure on the button and the air horn would go off.

The next bit was trickier. We strung a string above the toilet, so the tub of insects could be hung in mid-air over the seat. It was quite hard to get it just right but we managed eventually. Then

and an old woman in front of us threw her egg sandwich in the air. Alan Alan, I'm afraid to say, accidentally let out a shock-fart, and the conductor told us off (for blasting the air horn, not for Alan Alan doing a fart – I'm not sure if you can get told off for doing a fart on public transport).

we sneaked out on to the landing and waited for my dad.

And waited.

The model train chugged its way up the stairs, weaving in and out of the bedrooms, before making its way back downstairs again.

But still no Dad.

At this rate, there wouldn't even be any insects left in the box, as they'd have eaten each other completely by the time he arrived.

Finally, we heard feet on the stairs. Quick as a flash, I dashed into the loo, peeled the lid off the insect tub and placed a piece of paper on top, praying it would be able to keep them inside for just long enough.

I lifted the toilet seat up so I didn't set off the air horn and jumped on to the edge of it, wobbling dangerously as I hung the insect tub on the string. Then I got down, carefully re-lowered the seat and ran out, just in the nick of time.

Alan Alan and I hid in my bedroom, peeping out as my dad walked into the toilet, newspaper under his arm. I held my breath, my heart pounding. Alan Alan gripped my hand in his sweaty paw.

The toilet door was shut, then locked.

For a moment, there was silence.

Then we heard the ear-piercing screech of the air horn as my dad sat down, followed immediately by an even more piercing scream, as my dad leaped up in shock, only to bang his head on the tub, spilling the insects all over himself.

He burst out of the bathroom, clutching his trousers and jumping around like he had ants in his pants. Which he probably did, to be honest. He also had some ladybirds, a centipede and a few spiders in his hair, plus a daddy-long-legs stuck to his face. The moth just flapped on the ground uselessly. I knew we shouldn't have bothered putting it in.

My dad ran straight past us down the stairs, waving his arms in the air and screaming. My dad was screaming! Athena's shock therapy was working! He bolted outside, Alan Alan and I close behind, and started flailing around, trying to wipe off all

the insects. Eventually he got rid of the last of them and stood panting.

I approached him, my nerves jangling. He glared at me, breathing hard. I could practically see steam coming out of his nostrils. He looked angrier than I had *ever* seen him.

Come on, Dad, I thought. *Please. Have a go at me. Be a normal dad.*

His lips twitched. I could almost see words forming.

Please, Dad!

Slowly, a worm crawled out of his left eyebrow and across his forehead. With a long, drawn-out breath, he pulled it off, stared at it sadly, then at me sadly and trudged back inside in silence.

We'd failed again. My eyes pricked with angry tears as I heard Alan Alan walk up behind me.

'Never mind, Uma,' he said. 'Next time it'll work. I'm sure of it.'

That's right, said Athena, who had been quiet for some time. **We were incredibly close. The next one should be enough to do it.**

And that meant it was time for the final, *ultimate* shock.

* * *

Now, you have to be very careful, whispered Athena into my ear.

'I know,' I said.

You CANNOT let Alan Alan anywhere near it, OK?

'I know!' I repeated. 'You've already told me loads of times!'

'What's she saying?' asked Alan Alan.

'Nothing!' I replied, perhaps a little too quickly.

'Ugh. Whenever you say that, it's always her being rude about me!' he said, showing a surprising amount of insight.

Do you promise you won't let him touch anything, no matter how much he asks? Because I'm ninety-three per cent certain he will ask.

'Yes!' I snapped. 'I promise!'

'Gah!' shouted Alan Alan. 'What do you have to promise?'

152

'Uhhh . . . she made me promise to tell you how much she has changed her opinion of you and how she really likes you now.'

That is a lie, Uma! Athena sounded genuinely shocked. *Please tell Alan Alan the truth IMMEDIATELY!*

'Aww,' said Alan Alan. 'That's really nice. Thanks, Athena!'

Ugh, said Athena. *Unbelievable.*

We were down in the basement. I was pretty sure we weren't allowed to be in here. Dad had put a big sign on the basement door with a picture of a child in a crossed-out circle, which I *guessed* meant that children weren't allowed. But, really, who knows? I couldn't be *one hundred per cent* certain, so we had ignored it and, the moment Dad had gone upstairs, we'd opened the door (which obviously creaked at super-max volume), sneaked in and tiptoed down the stairs.

In front of us, in the middle of a great city surrounded by mountains, was the control centre for Dad's whole train set. Hundreds of bewildering knobs and buttons stretched out in three great panels.

Athena had told us to look out for a series of black boxes, each one the size of a punnet of strawberries. We saw them in the corner: the batteries. Eight of them in a row, connected by wires, powered the whole train set which snaked its way through the basement and up the stairs to the rest of the house.

From my pocket, I pulled out the wire and clips we had bought on our shopping trip.

Gently, whispered Athena.

Just as I had been instructed, I gingerly bent down to connect the wire to the top of a battery using a metal clip. When it successfully clipped on, I gasped in relief.

Now you have to attach the other end to the track, whispered Athena. **This is the really dangerous part.**

Swallowing nervously, I held the wire and clip in my trembling hands and leaned towards the train track.

'Uma,' whispered Alan Alan.

'What?'

'I think I should do this bit.'

'*What?*' I said, turning to glare at him.

'It looks, you know, a bit dangerous, so maybe I should help? I have training – bomb disposal.'

There is no *way* he had training.

No, groaned Athena. *Don't let him!*

'It's fine, thank you,' I said to Alan Alan. 'I can manage.'

'I know you can manage,' Alan Alan said. 'But I'm a *professional*, Uma.'

Athena hissed. *DO NOT LET HIM! HE WILL MESS IT UP AND ELECTROCUTE US ALL!*

I had to think fast. 'I can't let you take that risk,' I said.

'But –'

'And it's my dad, Alan Alan. I need to be the one who shocks him. I need to be the one who makes him talk.'

After a few seconds of hard thought, Alan Alan nodded and stepped back. Athena let out a sigh of relief. I went back to work, and slowly, slowly, slowly brought the clip and wire to the track.

Now clip it on but, whatever you do, do NOT touch the track after it's connected.

I took one final breath, held it, steadied my hand and then gently clipped the wire to the track. Yes!

Immediately, I heard a new soft humming, the sound of electrical current from the row of batteries passing through the track. It had worked. The track was electrified!

I ran up to the hall and placed a plastic straw on the track, jamming it in but being extra careful not to touch the buzzing metal with my fingers, and we ran off to hide. A moment later, one of Dad's trains trundled round the corner, hit the straw and immediately derailed, clattering to the floor.

My dad had ears like a bat when it came to the train set. I'd once accidentally stood on a tiny plastic tree while getting out of the bath and my dad heard the snap all the way down in the sitting room, and came running in to inspect the damage.

Sure enough, within a few seconds, my dad came clomping down the stairs to see what was going on. From behind the kitchen door, Alan Alan and I were able to see the track and the derailed train lying on its side on the floor.

Dad appeared, his brow furrowed, and he bent over and picked up the train. This was it. It was now or never. He carefully placed the train back on the track, then spotted the plastic straw. He tried to tug it free, but I had wedged it very tightly. Dad leaned over further and really pulled at the straw, but it held fast. Finally, Dad put his hands on either side of the track – and touched the rails.

The effect was extraordinary and immediate. Dad started making screeching noises like an owl with a firework up its backside. Sparks shot out of the end of the train and Dad's hair stood on end.

'Hoooooooooh-hooo-hooooheeeeeeee!' Dad screamed.

It was working! I jumped and whooped.

'HOOWAGGGGHHHHHAHHHH!' my dad screamed, as he jerked and flapped. The track was fizzing and humming sharply. I could smell burning but I didn't care! It was working!

'*HAAAAAARGHHHHEEEEEEEEEE!*' Dad gave a final screech and managed to pull himself away from the track. He collapsed on to his back, gasping and staring at the ceiling.

I walked over and stood looking down at him. He turned his eyes to me, still breathing hard. He had a little bit of drool coming out of his mouth.

'Hello, Dad,' I said, smiling.

'Wha-wha-wha–' he stuttered, his eyes burning. 'Wha-whargh-bah!'

'Go on, Dad! What do you want to say?' I beamed, my eyes filling with tears.

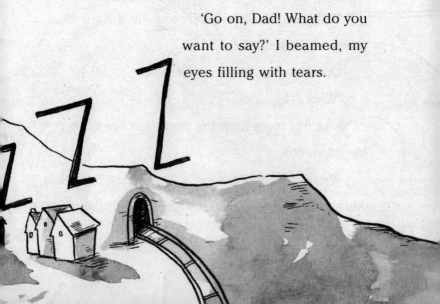

Sensing the moment of success was at hand, Alan Alan stepped behind me. And trod on one of the spiders we had used earlier. He squashed it all over the bottom of his shoe and Alan Alan slipped straight over, his glasses flying off and his hand grabbing at the nearest thing to break his fall.

The still-electrified train track.

Alan Alan's scream was much more high-pitched than Dad's – more like the sound a piglet might make if it was being chased by a tyrannosaurus rex. And, just like Dad, his hair stood on end, and he jerked and flapped. What didn't happen to Dad but *did* happen to Alan Alan was this: his eyebrows caught fire. Both of them.

'AIIIIIEIEIIEIEIIIIEIEEEE!' screamed Alan Alan, pretty understandably.

Quickly, said Athena. *Kick him!*

'What?' I gasped.

Kick him away from the track! You need to break the connection!

Without thinking, I did a flying kick into Alan Alan and knocked him across the floor. We both landed in a great heap. I jumped up and started batting at his face, putting out the flames. There was not much eyebrow left, though – just a few ashy, curled-up stubs of hair.

Alan Alan felt what was left of them and whimpered.

'My eyebrows . . . They're *gone*. They've been completely fried.'

He wasn't wrong.

Then Dad sat bolt upright. He stared at me. I mean, *really* stared at me. And then he roared. Like a proper huge angry lion that had just been electrocuted. He pointed a finger at me and roared again. He stood up on wobbly legs, holding himself steady on the wall. Then, with one last roar of fury, he stormed off.

We'd nearly done it. *Nearly*. But that was it now. The end of the plan. We had no more shocks to give him.

Athena had failed.

I was never going to get my dad back.

It was time to give up.

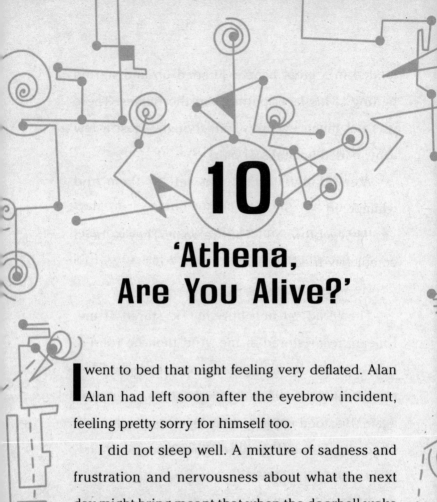

10

'Athena, Are You Alive?'

I went to bed that night feeling very deflated. Alan Alan had left soon after the eyebrow incident, feeling pretty sorry for himself too.

I did not sleep well. A mixture of sadness and frustration and nervousness about what the next day might bring meant that when the doorbell woke me the next morning I felt like I'd only had about half an hour's sleep. I popped Athena into my ear groggily.

Good morning, Uma. Just to warn you, Alan Alan is at the door and he has done something . . . unexpected.

'Don't worry,' I said as I trundled down the stairs to open the front door, 'I always expect the unexpected where Alan Alan is – HOLY MARY, MOTHER OF GOD, WHAT HAVE YOU DONE TO YOURSELF, ALAN ALAN?'

I don't even know where the phrase 'Holy Mary, Mother of God' came from; I think my dad used to say it back before Mum died. It just sort of fell out of my mouth. Because Alan Alan had indeed done something . . . unexpected.

'I don't know what you're talking about,' Alan Alan said innocently.

'Your . . . your . . . *eyebrows* . . .' I said, not believing what I was seeing.

'Oh! *That*. I thought I looked a bit weird without them, so I trimmed some hair off Dolly Barkon and glued them where my eyebrows should be.'

'YOU DID WHAT?'

oh, THAT...

'I trimmed some hair off Dolly and made some eyebrows out of it.'

'YOU MADE FAKE EYEBROWS OUT OF YOUR DOG'S FUR?'

'They look good, right? You can hardly tell the difference.'

I was lost for words. His eyebrows were so *long*. And so *curly*.

'Yeah. They look . . . um . . . perfectly normal,' I lied unconvincingly.[13] But if Alan Alan noticed me being unconvincing, he ignored it.

'Anyway, I'm not here to talk about eyebrows all day,' said Alan Alan, crossing his arms. 'I'm here to talk about breaking into Minerva.'

I have to admit I was pretty relieved to be changing the subject. Although I still couldn't take my eyes off them, fluttering gently in the breeze from the open window . . . I quickly pulled Alan Alan inside, shut the door and closed the window.

'Before we start, though, I have a number of questions I'd like to ask Athena,' Alan Alan continued.

---

[13] You see – I told you I only ever lie for good reasons.

OK, said hologram-Athena, suddenly appearing next to us. **I can predict exactly what you will ask –**

'Oh, don't even start with your prediction stuff!' interrupted Alan Alan. 'Because of your predictions, I have no eyebrows!'

For the first time ever, Athena didn't answer back.

'Firstly, why did the electricity burn off my eyebrows and not Uma's dad's? His are *way* bushier than mine.'

Correct. However, you had sticky juice from Ultra-Sour Face-Scrunching Gobstoppers all over your face. Combined with the sugar powder from Super-Orangey Orangutan Bumslaps, the juice created a highly unstable compound more flammable than jet fuel. When combined with electricity, the result was . . . explosive.

Alan Alan looked a little shamefaced. 'Well . . . why didn't you tell me to wash my face?' he snapped.

I did not think it necessary as I had underestimated your clumsiness levels. I shall update my systems.

Alan Alan sniffed. 'Couldn't you have tried cutting the power when you saw I was being shocked?'

The wiring in this house is eighty-three years old. I was worried it would backfire and fry my circuitry.

'Hmm,' said Alan Alan, narrowing his eyes, which should have made him look like he was suspicious, but with his new extra-long-and-curly dog-hair eyebrows just looked hilarious. 'So it's not fine for your circuitry to be fried but OK for my eyebrows?'

I could have died, Athena replied flatly.

'What do you mean, you "could have died"?' shouted Alan Alan. 'YOU CAN'T DIE BECAUSE YOU'RE NOT ALIVE!'

A silence swamped the room, thick as tar.

'Alan Alan,' I said. 'That's not very nice. Say you're sorry to Athena.'

Athena looked down, so we couldn't see her face. **There's no need to apologize. He's right. I'm not alive. Not like you.**

I didn't know what to say to that, so I didn't say anything.[14] But then I thought of how I would feel if she had been destroyed. 'Athena, you might not be the same as us but you *are* alive. I think so, anyway.'

Athena looked at me and gave a small smile. 'Thank you,' she whispered.

'Well, all right then,' Alan Alan said. 'Next question. Why didn't your plan work? Why should we trust you to help us break into Minerva when you can't even get one man talking again?'

I nearly did. If we keep it up –

14 I think more people should try this. Too many people speak when they have nothing to say.

'If we keep it up at this rate, we'll kill him! Or ourselves!'

I felt the same anger as Alan Alan, the same frustration that the plan hadn't worked, but I also felt sorry for Athena. She looked crestfallen.

'Maybe we should give my dad a break?' I suggested gently.

Alan Alan grunted in agreement.

Very well. We will suspend that plan for the moment. Athena looked up. **It's time to steal the alpacas.**

And although deep down I knew the plan to break into Minerva and save the village was almost certainly doomed to fail, I felt my heart flutter with excitement. Anything to distract us from the failure with my dad. Something was bothering me, though.

'But, Athena . . . isn't it wrong to steal?'

Good question, Uma. There is a branch of philosophy called utilitarianism that –

'You-Tilly what-now?' interrupted Alan Alan.

Utilitarianism. It means doing the most amount of good for the most amount of people.

'Oh, *that*!' Alan Alan laughed unconvincingly. 'I knew that. I just misheard you, that's all.'

Athena glanced at me and raised an eyebrow. **So**, she continued, **in this case, the good that we do by saving the village will outweigh any bad that we might be doing by stealing the alpacas.**

'OK, but that won't stop us getting in trouble,' I said. 'Won't Old Mr McIntosh call the police?'

Mr McIntosh is drunk seventy-three point six per cent of the time, Athena said. **Furthermore, his alpacas have escaped thirty-eight times already this year, causing the police to be called out nineteen times. I calculate there is a ninety-eight point seven per cent chance the police will not believe Mr McIntosh if he tells them that some children have stolen his alpacas. Especially as he has already told the police that three times this month.**

'Now *that* is brilliant!' I clapped. 'Foolproof!'

Even Alan Alan had to grudgingly agree. 'So, when do we do it?' he asked.

Now!

We both jumped to our feet, all thought of failure gone from our minds.

And, Uma?

'Yes?'

Fetch the lunch boxes.

* * *

Twenty-five minutes later, we were walking to Old Mr McIntosh's farm, both carrying My Little Pony lunch boxes packed with tuna sandwiches, apples, bags of crisps and smoothie cartons.

'So *that's* why we needed these?' Alan Alan asked huffily. 'To carry a *packed lunch*?'

It is important to have a sensible lunch to maintain optimal blood sugar levels, Athena said through her little speaker.

'So that's *it*? *That's* the reason?' snapped Alan Alan.

I had to admit I agreed with Alan Alan – I was preeetty disappointed with that.

I might have a further reason for the lunch boxes

that will be revealed later.

'Rubbish!' barked Alan Alan. 'You're making this up as you go along!'

'Maybe we should trust Athena?' I said uncertainly.

'Maybe you should trust *me* when I say this is a terrible plan and it's going to get us in dire trouble?' muttered Alan Alan.

I knew he had a point. The plan was almost one hundred per cent unlikely to work, and one hundred per cent likely to get us in trouble. But when I thought about my silent dad and the idea of losing our home, I found I didn't care. Sometimes, no matter the odds, you just have to do *something*. It's better to try and fail than do nothing at all. Even if there was only half a per cent chance of succeeding.

'Why did they have to be My Little Pony lunch boxes, anyway?' Alan Alan was still seething. 'Why not plain ones?'

Because My Little Pony is your favourite.

'*What?*' Alan Alan squawked.

The last lunch box your parents bought you was a My Little Pony one.

'I WAS SIX!' Alan Alan shouted. 'I haven't liked My Little Pony for years!'

Athena was silent for a moment. But you still like My Little Pony, Uma?

'I do not!' I lied.[15] I'm not quite sure *why* I lied

---

[15] OK, I didn't have a good reason for lying here. But at least I'm telling the truth about that, all right?

but I just didn't want Alan Alan to know I still liked them. I couldn't help but wonder if Alan Alan was telling the truth either.

I see. I shall update my systems.

There was something in Athena's voice, though, that made me think that perhaps she had known all along and was just getting amusement from it. But then I decided I had to be imagining that.

'I thought you were supposed to know everything already!' Alan Alan said.

I know ALMOST everything. I know ninety-nine point eight per cent of all knowable information.

'And what's the point two per cent you don't know?' I asked.

I refuse to learn about celebrity gossip. Or the names of YouTubers.

That was fair enough.

We fell silent, lost in our thoughts. Although it was still quite early, the sun was blasting down. Geoff, the village peacock, was strutting along a half-broken moss-covered wall beside the road and shook his feathers at us as we passed.

Athena suddenly spoke. My satellites are picking something up.

'Like what?' I asked.

Like trouble.

'What do you mean, trouble?'

Athena paused for a second. Then: You need to run.

'What?'

Run!

'Run where?' I asked, panic starting to rise.

Anywhere!

We started running, our lunch boxes banging

against our knees, towards Old Mr McIntosh's farm.

Not that way!

We U-turned and started running in the opposite direction, back down the lane to my house.

'Uma,' panted Alan Alan. 'There's someone after us.'

I took a quick look over my shoulder. It was Lexie, closely followed by Stephanie Vee. They were on their bikes, pedalling furiously straight towards us.

Quickly! Into the field!

We careered off the road into the field, just in time to see Luigseach-Meadhbh[16] McLoughlin and Madeleine

[16] OK – this is how you pronounce it. It sounds like Loosha-Mave.

Gilligan pedalling over the brow of the hill right in front of us.

'By Jove, they've caught us in a pincer movement,' exclaimed Alan Alan, with a touch more admiration in his voice than I was comfortable with.

'Come on!' I yelled.

We turned right and sprinted into a patch of longer grass that slowed down the chasing bikes. We were doing it! We were getting away! What happened next was quite spectacular really.

Alan Alan was just ahead of me. Turning to check on our pursuers, he caught his foot on a root and flipped head over heels, sweets flying out of his many pockets. I tripped over one of his flailing feet and went flying straight over him, and we both ended up in a tangled heap of arms, legs and lunch boxes.

Lexie and her crew jumped off their bikes and surrounded us, grinning. We were trapped.

I sprang to my feet and squared up to Lexie. 'What do *you* want?' I tried to sound as brave as I could. I don't think it worked.

'Oh, not much,' said Lexie, circling me. 'Just – WHAT IS WRONG WITH HIS FACE?' she suddenly shouted, pointing at Alan Alan in horror.

Alan Alan looked behind him to see who Lexie was pointing at, saw there was nobody there and realized she meant him.

'What do you mean?' said Alan Alan, confused.

Lexie took a hasty step back as Alan Alan furrowed his terrifying eyebrows.

'Your *eyebrows*,' Lexie said, still pointing. 'WHAT'S HAPPENING WITH YOUR *EYEBROWS*?'

Alan Alan's hand shot up to his face. 'I don't know what you're talking about. There's absolutely nothing happening with my eyebrows. They're perfectly normal.'

'Perfectly normal? Those . . . *things*?' Lexie said, shaking her head in disbelief. 'Whatever. We aren't here to talk about those mutant caterpillars. You've got something we want. And I'm not talking about your My Little Pony lunch boxes.'

The four of them laughed at that and Alan Alan blushed furiously.

'I'm talking about something worth a lot of money,' Lexie said, grinning.

'What do you mean?'

I was suddenly grabbed from behind by Madeleine and Luigseach-Meadhbh. I struggled but I couldn't get away from their tight grip.

'So we bumped into that Stella Daw woman this morning,' Lexie said. 'And she told us you stole something from her. And that if we got it back from you, she'd give us fifty quid. Each.'

I swallowed, my mouth dry. 'I haven't got anything of hers.'

My words sounded hollow even to me.

'Ha! Really?' Lexie laughed. 'She told me it was a Bluetooth earpiece. A bit like that one you're wearing.'

Oh dear, said Athena. *Goodbye, Uma.*

And then Lexie ripped Athena from my ear.

I cried out and desperately struggled in vain to get away from the vice-like grip of Luigseach-Meadhbh and Madeleine, lashing out at Lexie with thrashing kicks. It was hopeless, though. Lexie just elbowed me in the stomach and I fell to the ground,

winded. The gang jumped on their bikes and started
pedalling.

Alan Alan ran after them but Luigseach-Meadhbh,
with a huge swing, full-on punched him right in the
face. He fell forward on to his hands and knees,
and, before I could stop her, Lexie jumped off her
bike and booted Alan Alan right on the backside,
sending him sprawling into the dirt.

Luigseach-Meadhbh started shaking her hand vigorously – one of Alan Alan's fake eyebrows was now stuck to her. Finally, it came flying off and landed in the grass. Then they all jumped back on their bikes and rode off, whooping and cheering.

I had never felt so alone. My mum gone, my dad still miserable and silent. And now my best friend sitting on his bum with a bleeding nose and Athena snatched away – all because of me.

I'd promised Athena that I'd keep her safe and now Lexie was going to give her to Stella Daw, who was going to wipe her memory. The thought of losing Athena forever broke my heart. I wanted to give up – just lie on the ground and never get up again.

So it was a bit of a surprise when Alan Alan mopped up his bloody nose on his camouflage T-shirt, wiped the rest of the blood away with the back of his arm and said, sounding surprisingly jolly, 'Come on, then.'

'What do you mean, "Come on, then"? We're finished. It's over.'

'*What?*' Alan Alan gave me a surprised look (although because he was missing an eyebrow, all his looks were surprised now). 'Are you saying we just lie in this field and give up? I didn't get where I am today by *giving up*!'

I wanted to say: 'Alan Alan, what are you talking about? You're knocked on your backside, with a bloody nose and one properly disturbing eyebrow made out of dog hair.' But I didn't. What I *did* say was: 'Yes, let's just lie in this field and give up.'

Alan Alan jumped to his feet with surprising agility, speed and confidence, considering he'd just been knocked clean off them. He bent down and picked up his other eyebrow and stuck it back on. Then he held his hand out to me.

'The battle may have been lost but the war is far from over, Uma. Together we're going to get your dad back, save the village *and* get revenge on that gang of losers while we're at it. But first we get Athena back. You with me?'

I looked at Alan Alan's brave, bloodied and still quite surprised-looking face, and my heart swelled.

I grinned and grabbed his hand. He pulled me to my feet.

'Let's do it!' I said, bursting with new-found confidence.

'Let's do it!' echoed Alan Alan, high-fiving me. 'How *do* we do that, then?'

11

'Athena, Can Dogs Feel Embarrassed?'

'**I**'ve absolutely no idea,' I said, my new-found confidence disappearing as quickly as it had appeared.

'Well, we need a plan,' Alan Alan replied. 'Our combat operations need to be mapped out with needle-like precision down to the very last detail.'

'I guess we . . . uhh . . . find Lexie and her gang and, um, somehow get Athena back from them,' I said uncertainly.

'Brilliant!' said Alan Alan. 'You're a tactical genius!'

Am I? I thought.

'So, where do you think they've gone?' continued Alan Alan.

Now *that* I did know. There was only one place they would have gone.

Badger's Hole, I thought. 'Badger's Hole,' I said.

'Badger's Hole . . .' Alan Alan echoed with an air of awe.

'Badger's Hole,' I repeated – unnecessarily, but liking the sense of mystery it gave. Badger's Hole was the place in the woods where Lexie and her gang had their den. They were *always* there. That's where they would have gone while they waited to make contact with Stella Daw.

'Let's go, then!' Alan Alan shouted. 'What are we waiting for?'

'What are we waiting for?' I asked in disbelief. 'How about any idea at all of what we are going to do when we get there? There's more of them than us. *And* they just totally kicked our butts.'

'That's mere trifling detail!' said Alan Alan. 'Real soldiers have to think on their feet, under the white-hot pressure of battle. Come on – we haven't a moment to lose!'

I shook my head, a rueful smile on my face. I had to admire his blind bravery in the face of the obvious facts. 'OK, then,' I said. 'Will you be able to keep up? You know I'm school cross-country champion!'

'Don't you worry,' said Alan Alan. 'I've been doing high-intensity training.'

I started running, setting a fierce pace. Lexie's lot had a head start on us and Badger's Hole was on the other side of the village. Forty seconds later, I noticed Alan Alan wasn't next to me. I turned to see him stopped ten metres back, bent over, panting, hands on his thighs.

'I'm . . . sorry,' he gasped. 'You're . . . so . . . fast.'

'I thought you said you'd been doing high-intensity training?'

'I have,' wheezed Alan Alan. 'But over short distances. I haven't progressed to the high-intensity programme for long distances. Would you mind if we walked very fast instead? I'm a highly trained fast walker.'

So we walked quickly to Badger's Hole instead of running. And *that's* why we arrived too late and *that's* how Stella Daw got Athena back.

Or so I thought.

* * *

'You're too late!' Lexie sneered. 'We gave it to that woman and she left about ten minutes ago. And we're rich!'

We hadn't even made it as far as Badger's Hole. Lexie and her gang were loitering on the outskirts of the wood when we walked very fast up to them.

'*Ha ha ha, you're too late!*' laughed Lexie.

'HA HA HA, YOU'RE TOO LATE!' laughed Luigseach-Meadhbh, repetitively.

'YOU'RE TOO LATE, HA HA HA!' laughed Stephanie, who at least tried to mix it up a bit.

'HA HA HA!' laughed Madeleine, who I think wasn't sure exactly what she was supposed to be laughing at.

We didn't need telling, though. We had lost

Athena. Stella Daw was probably wiping her memory at that very moment. My head told me that Athena wasn't really alive, not like people are, but I couldn't bear to think about her last few moments. Could she feel fear? Would she feel alone? In my heart I knew she would.

And in my heart I knew that losing Athena meant losing the only hope of helping my dad and saving the village too. And that meant losing Alan Alan as well. It was all too much; I started crying.

'Aww, look at her! So sad! BOO HOO HOO!' gloated Stephanie.

'Leave her alone!' Alan Alan shouted. 'Or you're in big trouble.'

This was wildly overconfident talk from someone who, less than half an hour ago, had had his butt kicked. Literally.

'OOOH, SCARY!' sniggered Lexie. 'Do you want Luigseach-Meadhbh to knock yer dog-hair eyebrows off again?'

I couldn't bear to see Alan Alan hurt any more, not after everything else. I placed my hand on his arm.

'Come on,' I said quietly. 'Let's just go.'

Alan Alan glared at them one last time, and then we turned and walked away, our heads held high but our ears ringing with the shouts and taunts that Lexie's gang howled at us.

We didn't say a word all the way home.

Finally, we reached our houses, and Alan Alan

turned to me. 'I'm sorry, Uma.'

'What for?'

'If I'd been able to run the whole way, we might have made it in time.'

'Don't be daft,' I said, doing my best to smile. 'It wasn't your fault.'

I mean, it was *totally* his fault, but there was no point dwelling on that.

'Thanks, Uma. You're right. I guess it was both our faults. Completely equal.'

'Yeah, I guess,' I said. 'Well . . . maybe not *completely* equal . . . Maybe like sixty–forty.'

'I KNEW YOU THOUGHT IT WAS MY FAULT!' Alan Alan shouted, storming down the path to his house. 'WELL, IF THAT'S THE WAY YOU FEEL, MAYBE I SHOULD JUST –'

And that's when it hit me. 'WAIT!' I shouted.

'WAIT, WHAT?' Alan Alan shouted back.

'They knew about your eyebrows!'

'So what? Why are you bringing *that* up again? I mean –'

'Think!' I interrupted, excitement pumping

through me. 'They called them "dog-hair eyebrows".
How did they know they were made of Dolly Barkon's
fur?'

'I dunno,' Alan Alan shrugged.

'Exactly! They couldn't *possibly* know that. *We*
are the only ones who knew and *we* definitely didn't
mention it! So who do you think told them?'

'Dolly told them?' Alan Alan gasped, his eyes
wide with shock.

'DOLLY TOLD THEM!? ARE YOU COMPLETELY
– No! How could a dog tell them? Never mind. NO
– *Athena told them!*'

'Ohhh, yeah . . . That makes much more sense.'

'Obviously they'll have put

Athena in their ears to see what all the fuss about an earpiece was, and if Athena has been talking to them, she'll have told them how she knows everything. And if they know *that*, there's no way they'd give her to Stella Daw for a poxy fifty quid each.'

'Why not?'

'Think about it, Alan Alan! Lexie and her lot are always in trouble at school. Athena could give them the answer to every bit of homework! She could even tell them what was going to be in the tests! Even Lexie's not stupid enough to get rid of her, knowing that, so THEY MUST STILL HAVE HER!'

Alan Alan gasped for the second time in thirty seconds.

'We have to get her back!' My heart was thumping.

'YES!' cried Alan Alan, his eyes alive with excitement. 'But first let me sort out some new eyebrows, OK?'

'OK but be quick,' I said, and then, with a rush of blood to the head I would soon regret, added, 'LET'S GO TO WAR!'

Alan Alan stopped dead, his eyes unfocused.

'Yes,' he said gravely. 'We shall fight them on the beaches.'

I laughed a little uncertainly. 'Ha, yeah, I don't mean *actual* war. I –'

'We shall fight them in the fields,' he said, nodding.

I laughed again, even less certainly.

'We shall fight them in Badger's Hole. The time for speech is over. We shall settle this through fire and blood.' And then he turned and ran into his house, calling for Dolly, leaving me wondering whether I had lost one friend forever and had another go bonkers all in the same day.

I decided to pop in to see how Dad was getting on. I cracked open my front door. The house was as silent as ever.

'Hi, Dad!' I called.

A single grunt came in reply.

Dad was sitting at the kitchen table, tinkering with one of the model trains. He glared at me as I came in – he clearly hadn't forgiven me for the electrocution. Or the insects. Or the mice. Thinking about it, I'd probably made him even less likely to talk to me after all that. And I'd be glaring at me too.

I poured myself a glass of squash and sat anxiously waiting for Alan Alan until finally the doorbell rang. I opened the door and standing before me was the most – and this is a mega-whopper of an understatement – surprising sight.

It was Alan Alan, once again head to toe in camouflage gear, but this time he also had his face painted with green war-stripes across his cheeks and forehead and it looked like he had leaves stuck in his hair. He had a huge bag over his shoulder and Dolly next to him on a lead.

I suppose I could have asked him what was in the bag. Or why his face was painted green or why he'd chosen to put dandelion leaves in his hair. I probably *should* have suggested he needed to calm down a bit on the whole 'going to war' vibe. But no – what I *did* say was: 'WHAT HAVE YOU DONE TO DOLLY?'

And why did I say this? Because Dolly had no eyebrows. Let me repeat that: *Dolly Barkon had no eyebrows*. Instead she had two bald strips where her eyebrows should have been. Alan Alan had been making his *fake* eyebrows out of Dolly's *actual* eyebrows. I suggest you take a moment to re-read that last sentence and take it in properly.

'What?' asked Alan Alan.

'Why did you have to use her eyebrows?' I bellowed.

'What else should I have done?' asked Alan Alan, genuinely mystified.

'Could you not have taken the hair from somewhere less . . . obvious?' I asked, still gobsmacked.

'That wouldn't have been as realistic, though, would it?' Alan Alan said slowly, like he was explaining something incredibly simple to a small child.[17] 'Besides, she's a dog. She doesn't know she looks a bit odd.'

One glance at Dolly told me that she knew *exactly* how she looked. 'Anyway,' I said, trying to get back to the plan. 'What's in the bag?'

---

[17] I mean, I am quite a small child but I'm not a *stupid* small child.

'Top secret.'

'What do you mean, "top secret"?'

'It means I can't tell you. It's on a need-to-know basis – and you don't need to know.'

'Well, I am part of the plan, so I actually do need to know, don't I?'

Alan Alan sighed. 'What have I got in here? Vengeance. That's what I've got in here. And we will have our vengeance, in this life or the next.'

'OK, you're starting to freak me out now.'

Alan Alan saluted, gave a smart about-turn and marched down the garden path with Dolly in tow.

What else could I do? I followed, of course. Athena needed us.

* * *

We hopped on our bikes – Alan Alan struggled a bit with all the stuff he was carrying – and set off.

The sun was beginning to set, but it was still warm out and every so often we'd pass somebody who would look (quite reasonably, I felt) somewhat startled to see a girl cycling through the village with a boy dressed like he was off to fight a jungle war and a permanently surprised-looking eyebrowless dog. I mean, I'd stop and stare at that.

A few minutes later, we entered the woods.

'Right,' whispered Alan Alan. 'From here on, we employ maximum stealth.'

I nodded. 'Maximum stealth, OK, Dolly?' Dolly stared blankly at Alan Alan. Or maybe she stared nervously, wondering if Alan Alan was going to shave her again – I couldn't tell.

We parked our bikes and crept forward, all three of us employing absolute maximum stealth, until we approached Lexie's den. We could hear them – Lexie, Stephanie, Luigseach-Meadhbh and Madeleine – laughing and yelping, way before we could see them.

Alan Alan crouched down, whipped a pair of binoculars out of his bag and passed them to me. I peered through them – there was Badger's Hole, a round dip in the middle of the wood that Lexie's gang had fenced off with logs and sticks. They had

197

attached pirate flags to the fence, and there were

thorny sticks sticking out of the ground all around

it, so if you weren't careful and stood on one, it

hurt your foot a bit. It was all very intimidating.

I focused the binoculars on Lexie and, sure

enough, at her left ear was a little glimmer of white.

'It's Athena!' I whispered excitedly. 'Lexie's

wearing Athena! I knew it!'

Alan Alan nodded solemnly. 'And now we unleash

hell.' Reaching into his army bag, Alan Alan pulled

out a huge drone. Dangling beneath it were what

looked like four . . . 'Electric razors!' said Alan Alan, a wild look in his eye.

'Electric razors,' I repeated uncertainly.

Dolly whimpered nervously.

'It was doing Dolly's eyebrows that gave me the idea!' he said, the look in his eye getting even wilder. One by one, he flicked all the razors on and they hummed like a swarm of bees. Then he pressed a button on a small remote control and the drone whirred into life. Dolly growled at it.

'Shush, Dolly! MAXIMUM stealth!' Alan Alan warned. Then he pressed another button and the drone took off into the air.

Dolly, completely forgetting the maximum stealth, gave an uncertain yelp. And that was enough to make Lexie and her gang look round.

'It's now or never!' I said.

'Go, go, go!' cried Alan Alan, and we burst out from our cover, the drone soaring over our heads to hover above the gang, who glanced nervously upwards, trying to work out exactly what was happening.

'What do you nerds want?' snapped Madeleine.

'And what's this thing doing?' asked Luigseach-Meadhbh, peering at the drone.

'You'll find out if you don't give us that back,' I said, pointing at Lexie's ear.

Lexie just gave us an evil-looking grin. 'Athena,' she said. 'Tell me what these numbskulls are planning.'

We waited, holding our breath.

'Athena? ATHENA?! Ugh, what a time for the stupid thing to start updating!'

I smiled inside when I heard that. 'Hand her over, Lexie!' I said. 'Or else.'

'Or else *what*?' she replied, jutting her jaw defiantly.

'Or else THIS!' Alan Alan hollered.

He clicked a button and the drone swooped down. The razors hit Lexie's head with a short buzzing noise and Alan Alan pulled the drone back up out of reach.

Lexie's hands shot to her head and a look of horror crossed her face. The drone had shaved a great stripe right down the middle of her head.

Long strands of hair fluttered to the ground.

'NOOOOOOO!' she screamed. 'What have you done?'

But Alan Alan didn't stop there. He immediately started dive-bombing the others, who scattered in terror, screaming. I have to say, he had a terrifying aim. Despite the four of them running in all directions, he was merciless. Again and again he swooped the drone down, buzz-cutting great lumps out of their hair.

'Ha ha!' he whooped as one of Madeleine's plaits fell into a patch of nettles. 'Woo-hoo!' he roared as Stephanie's glossy fringe got shortened to all the way up her forehead.

I would have to have a long chat with Alan Alan about his behaviour once this was over. But until then I just had to stand back and admire his skill.

One by one, he got Lexie and her gang, swinging the drone down and herding them like terrified sheep. Dolly got involved too, growling and snapping if any of them tried to get too near to us.

'Make it stop!' Luigseach-Meadhbh howled.

But Alan Alan didn't.

'OK!' screamed Lexie. 'OK! You can have the stupid thing back! It doesn't even work any more!'

Alan Alan hovered the drone right over her head as she walked slowly over to me, pulled Athena from her ear and passed her back.

It felt so good feeling her in my hand again. I placed her gently in my ear. And straight away . . .

Hello, Uma.

I nearly burst into happy tears right there and then but we still had to get away. We edged backwards out of the den, the drone and Dolly keeping the four bullies at bay. Finally, when there was enough distance between us, Alan Alan let the drone drop

into his hands. We ran to our
bikes, then pedalled as fast
as we could out through the
woods and back to the road.

I turned round to check
where Alan Alan was. He was just behind me,
pedalling as fast as he could. But there in the
distance was a sight that turned my blood cold.
A black car speeding towards us.

It was Stella Daw and she was closing
in on us fast.

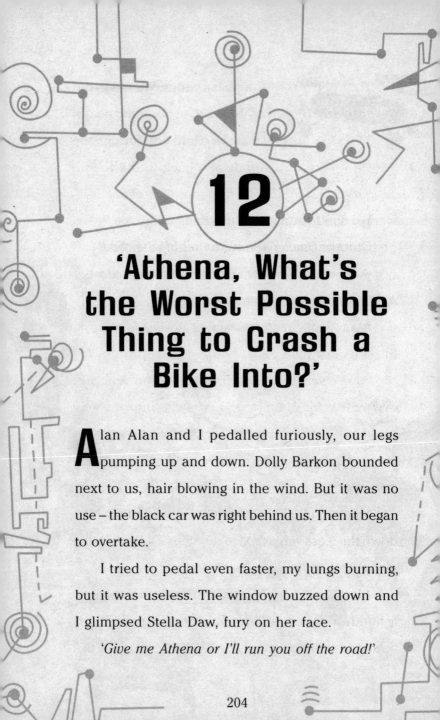

12

'Athena, What's the Worst Possible Thing to Crash a Bike Into?'

Alan Alan and I pedalled furiously, our legs pumping up and down. Dolly Barkon bounded next to us, hair blowing in the wind. But it was no use – the black car was right behind us. Then it began to overtake.

I tried to pedal even faster, my lungs burning, but it was useless. The window buzzed down and I glimpsed Stella Daw, fury on her face.

'Give me Athena or I'll run you off the road!'

Then she jerked the steering wheel and veered towards me. I swerved out of the way but nearly crashed into Alan Alan, who turned his bike away just in time.

'GIVE IT TO ME!'

We sped round a tight corner.

Quickly, Uma! You have to get off the road!

'Alan Alan!' I shouted. 'We have to get off the road!'

Alan Alan gave me a thumbs up. This was not his brightest idea as he totally lost control of his bike. He swerved to the right, then the left, and on to the – for Alan Alan, incredibly unfortunately placed – steep stone steps that led down to the high street. I heard a yelp of terror as he disappeared from sight.

I had no choice but to follow. I guided my bike down the grass verge next to the steps, Dolly skidding along next to me.

Alan Alan was bouncing down the steps at a hundred miles an hour, screaming as his tyres bounced on each step. 'NO-NO-NO-GA-GA-BA-BA-

HE-EE-ELP-ME-EE-EE!'

It was completely pointless him shouting that, as there was no one who could help. Nothing could stop him. Or nearly nothing.

Alan Alan shot off the bottom of the steps, still completely out of control, and straight down the high street, sending people diving out of the way in terror.

So it was terrible, terrible timing for my headteacher, Mrs Fazackerley-Denbury-Broughton-Brown, to step out of the newsagent's and drop a mint imperial. As she set down her wicker basket and bent to pick it up, Alan Alan finally found his brakes and squeezed them hard. Unfortunately, he must have damaged his back brake as he went crashing down the steps, because only the front brake worked and he went flying over the handlebars.

Time seemed to slow as he soared through the air in a graceful curve – face-first into Mrs Fazackerley-Denbury-Broughton-Brown's basket of evil chihuahuas.

The noise was dreadful. A chorus of snarling

and snapping that sounded even worse than our school's annual carol concert. Alan Alan pulled his head out of the basket screaming, with three chihuahuas clamped determinedly to his face. One had latched on to his nose, one was attached to an ear, and one was clinging on for dear life to Alan Alan's right cheek.

Alan Alan ran in circles, howling, flapping his arms wildly, trying to shake off the savage beasts until Mrs Fazackerley-Denbury-Broughton-Brown

hEY!

felled him with a brutal blow from her umbrella and began prising the snarling dogs off Alan Alan's face, one by one.

'Oh, my poor little angels! What has that nasty, horrible boy done to you!' she crooned as she dropped them delicately back into their basket.

I won't tell you what she then shouted at Alan Alan. It's not fit for a children's book and certainly not the sort of language a headteacher should use. Eventually, with a harrumph of disgust, she stalked away.

Once Alan Alan had picked himself up, dusted himself down and wiped his bleeding face, we looked around for Stella Daw and saw with some relief that we seemed to have given her the slip.

Satellite tracking indicates she is on the other side of the village, Athena said in my ear. *If you pedal straight home now, you should make it back in time.*

We jumped back on our bikes, and within a few minutes we were back in my bedroom.

Once I got my breath back, I grinned. Somehow, in some way, Alan Alan had done it. His plan had worked. I had Athena back. I gave Alan Alan the biggest hug.

'Well done!' I said, beaming. 'That razor-drone was amazing! Where did you get the idea?'

'I've been studying the tactics used by the Royal Air Force in the Battle of Britain.'

'They used drones with razors in the Second World War?' I asked.

'Not exactly . . .' said Alan Alan. 'But they *would* have done if they'd had the technology.'

'Well, anyway – the looks on their faces! It was brilliant, Alan Alan!'

Alan Alan blushed and saluted again. 'Just doing my duty, ma'am,' he said.

It was getting a bit late to try stealing the alpacas and breaking into Minerva again today and, anyway, Alan Alan wanted to do a bit of digging for the Tylney Treasure behind the Sheep's Cough before bed, so we agreed to meet first thing the next day. Alan Alan headed back to his house, Dolly barking at his heels, and I was alone again with Athena at last.

'Hello, Athena,' I said.

Hello, Uma.

'So how did you stop Lexie selling you to Stella Daw?'

I showed her a little bit of what I could do. Just enough to make sure she would want to keep me. Then I knew she would tell Stella she hadn't managed to steal me from you but I needed to send you a sign that Lexie still had me. So I told her about Alan Alan's dog-hair eyebrows. I knew she wouldn't be able to resist making fun of him to you about that. Well, I was ninety-three per cent certain.

'And you trusted me to be clever enough to work out your plan?'

I was ninety-nine per cent certain of that, Uma.

I grinned, lying back on my bed and looking up at the stick-on stars above me. It felt so good to have someone like Athena to talk to. She always made me feel better about myself.

I felt another question bubbling towards my mouth – the big question that normally sat in my brain like a coiled, black snake. But I couldn't find the right words. It was like the snake had wrapped itself around my tongue and wouldn't let me speak.

It's time for sleep now, Uma, continued Athena. *We have a big day tomorrow . . .*

* * *

The next thing I knew, my alarm was blaring. I turned it off and hopped out of bed. This was it. It was the day we were finally going to find out what Minerva were up to and hopefully – maybe – save the village.

It was seven o'clock and sunlight was already streaming through my curtains. By the time I had gobbled some breakfast, had a shower and brushed my teeth, Alan Alan was knocking on the door.

We sneaked out without seeing my dad, carrying the lunch boxes and tape, which Athena had insisted we bring.

A soft mist lay across Tylney, the steeple of the church looming out as if it floated on a cloud. With no distractions from Lexie or Stella Daw this time, it didn't take us long to reach Old Mr McIntosh's farm.

We could just about make out the alpacas on the far side of the field.

'OK, Athena, what do we do?' I asked.

What do we do about what?

'I *mean* what's our plan? You know – how do we get the alpacas drunk and steal them?'

I don't know.

'What do you mean, "I don't know"? It's –'

It was a joke. I am practising my humour. Did I succeed?

'Athena!' I spluttered. 'There's a time and a place!'

Understood. I shall update my time and place settings for humour. But, yes, I do have a plan. First,

we break into Mr McIntosh's farmhouse.

'OK . . . And is that safe?'

It measures twenty-three per cent on the safety–danger index.

I didn't know whether twenty-three per cent on the safety–danger index was good or not. It didn't *sound* particularly good.

Mr McIntosh is currently sound asleep. If we are fast and quiet, we should be fine.

'Old Mr McIntosh is asleep so we have to break in fast and quiet!' I repeated to Alan Alan, who nodded. He had a look on his face like he was trying to appear like he was listening but I'm not sure he was. He was eyeing the field of alpacas nervously.

'Got it,' he said. 'Go in fast and hard.'

'No!' I said. 'Fast and *quiet*, not fast and hard! Silently!'

Alan Alan nodded again. 'Yup, that's what I said,' he said. 'Never fear – I have been fully trained in silent infiltration. The trick is to keep calm under pressure and not to panic no matter what happens.'

Hmm, said Athena. *My suspicion levels have just leaped eighty-seven per cent.*

We hopped over the fence into Old Mr McIntosh's yard. A few startled-looking chickens scattered in surprise at the sudden intrusion.

Right, whispered Athena. *Go to the back door and try the latch.*

We followed her instructions, and our luck held – it was unlocked and the door creaked open.

Now go through the kitchen and turn right down the corridor.

We crept inside. Light struggled through the grimy windows. I thought we'd be stepping into silence, but we weren't.

Not by a long way.

There was a deafening rumble coming from deep in the house, so loud it was shaking the walls. It stopped for a moment and we held our breath. Then it started again, like an angry chainsaw.

It was Old Mr McIntosh's snoring.

You need to silently sneak past Mr McIntosh into the conservatory, which is on the other side of his sitting room. That's where he has his cider press.

We crept towards the sound, our fingers in our ears. It didn't take us long to locate the source of the dreadful racket. There, slouched in a patched-up old armchair, threadbare tartan rug on his lap, was Old Mr McIntosh, snoring away like a newborn baby.

A big, ugly seventy-year-old newborn baby with a wild grey mullet, hairy ears, false teeth dangling out of his mouth and a smell like a cabbage had come to life, farted, then died and then farted again.

We had to get past him, though. We had no choice.

I put a warning finger to my lips and pointed the way to Alan Alan. We tiptoed through the living room, past the snoring farmer and into a conservatory with broken windows that *stank* of rotten apples. In between the snores, which rattled the windows, we could hear the soft hum of wasps buzzing about the room. Lined up on the shelves was what we wanted: row after row of huge glass bottles full of honey-coloured cider. And next to the shelves a little trolley, which we could use to shift the bottles. Perfect.

We started loading the trolley as fast as we could, wincing at every clink the bottles made when they rattled against each other. We piled it as high as we dared.

You should not let Alan Alan push the trolley, Uma, Athena murmured in my ear. *There are –*

'I'll push!' hissed Alan Alan, grabbing the handle.

Before I could say a word, he began steering the trolley back into the sitting room, past the snoring Old Mr McIntosh.

I don't know if you have ever been to a cider mill but there's one thing that loves cider even more than farmers and alpacas do. And that is a wasp.

This was bad news.

Very bad news.

Because, as Alan Alan manoeuvred the trolley out of the conservatory, the wasps followed.

And I'm afraid to say that Alan Alan did not handle this well. I think he must have forgotten all his training in silent infiltration because, instead of staying calm under pressure, he panicked. He started jumping and flapping his hand around his head and pushing the trolley even faster, trying to escape the wasps, the bottles rattling and clinking noisily.

And then, at top speed, he bashed the trolley straight into the back of Old Mr McIntosh's chair.

'Wassafussawullawassa,' spluttered the old man, lifting his head and looking around.

Alan Alan and I ducked behind his chair and held our breath, not moving a muscle. One of the wasps decided to stop and have a rest too.

On the end of Alan Alan's nose.

Alan Alan's face froze in utter fear. He was completely cross-eyed, staring at the wasp. He let out a tiny whimper of terror.

I winced, praying that Old Mr McIntosh hadn't heard.

He muttered something about 'blasted turnips', slumped back in his chair and went silent. The wasp flew off the end of Alan Alan's nose and we slowly let out our breath . . . which turned out to be a bad idea, because right at that moment Old Mr McIntosh let rip with a *massive* trump. To say it felt like an earthquake would be an understatement. To say it smelled bad would be the understatement of the century.

It smelled like a dead yak that had lain out in the sun for a week.

Alan Alan looked at me again in panic, holding his nose. I desperately put a finger to my lips. It was like torture, sitting there in the stench, but we daren't move. I made a mental note that, if we got out of this alive, I would have stern words with Athena about why she hadn't warned us to buy gas masks.

Finally, we heard Old Mr McIntosh's rumbling snores start up again and we could escape the evil pong.

I glared at Alan Alan and grabbed the trolley off him.

He glared back, whispering, 'It wasn't my fault! Those wasps were about to sting me!'

'Some training!' I hissed back, and pushed the trolley out of the sitting room, through the kitchen and into the yard. We navigated it around to the back of the farmhouse and through the alpaca field to the water trough, terrified that each lump in the bumpy ground would cause the bottles to smash.

I rolled my sleeve up, stuck my hand into the trough and pulled the plug. We waited until all the water had drained, then I put the plug back in and we started refilling it with the cider. It stank – like apple juice mixed with vinegar and a sharp slap in the face. How anyone could drink it – even alpacas – was beyond me.

Pretty soon the trough was full to its brim. The alpacas were getting pretty curious about the two strangers in their field and had wandered over,

blinking their beautiful brown eyes. Head of the pack was the alpaca that Stella Daw had run over, the one with the blond mop of hair.

Alan Alan looked profoundly unhappy about this turn of events. 'I just *really* don't think alpacas are safe,' he said, edging away.

'Don't worry,' I said. 'They're basically just big goats.'

'Yes, but . . . I hate goats!' Alan Alan snapped.

'Why on earth do you hate goats?' I asked, baffled.

'I'm allergic. They make me sneeze.'

'OK but that's no reason to *hate* them. They're actually really lovely –'

'Fine, if you *really* want to know, a goat *killed* my Great-Aunt Mildred, THAT'S WHY!' Alan Alan blurted out.

Silence. Even the alpacas stood still, jaws open wide in shock.

'What?' I gasped.

What? said Athena. *I can find no record of a goat killing anyone in Alan Alan's family. According to the* Tylney Gazette, *his Great-Aunt Mildred was run over –*

'Yes! A goat killed her!' Alan Alan continued with a sob. 'Great-Aunt Mildred was minding her own business, walking home from the pub late one night, when a vicious goat jumped out from some bushes, bleating ferociously. The shock made her stumble backwards, straight into the path of a huge lorry. It flattened her like a pancake. The driver didn't see the goat but he rushed over to her, just in time to hear her dying words: "Billy . . . pushed me." You see! A billy goat pushed her! And *that's* why I don't like goats! Poor Great-Uncle William was never the same again. He was so sad he had to buy a Ferrari and move to Marbella with the lady next door.'

Silence fell on us once again, broken only by the sound of humming and squawking from the alpacas.[18]

Alan Alan looked like he was about to say something else but was interrupted by slurping as

---

[18] Yes, alpacas hum. They actually make the weirdest noises.

the alpacas started tucking into the super-strength cider in their trough.

'Well, they seem to like it,' said Alan Alan sullenly. He was right – half a dozen of them were lapping away, already starting to get feisty, grunting and hissing and shoving each other out of the way to get at the stinky drink.

Within minutes the cider was totally gone and the alpacas – well, the alpacas were totally drunk. Some were wandering around the field trying to *sing*. Some seemed to have lost control of their limbs and were stumbling all over the place. I'm afraid to say it even looked like one might have been being sick. He was certainly making a very strange noise in the corner of the field.

Great work! said Athena. *On to the next stage.*

'Which is?' I asked.

We steal Mr McIntosh's van.

'OK, right, we st– WHAT DID YOU SAY?!'

I thought I spoke perfectly clearly? I said –

'I heard you perfectly well the first time! But that is the most ridiculous plan yet! She wants us to steal Mr McIntosh's van!' I explained to Alan Alan, shaking my head in disbelief.

'Her electronics must have got fried,' said Alan Alan. 'Or maybe the cider fumes have got to her?'

'What on earth are you thinking, Athena? We can't even drive!'

I will instruct you. It's really quite simple.

Could an artificial intelligence lose its mind? It appeared so.

'Well,' said Alan Alan, 'I mean, we have half a dozen drunk alpacas – how are we supposed to get them to Minerva otherwise? A taxi isn't going to take them.'

Alan Alan had a point.

'OK,' I said, holding my hands up. 'If – and that's a ginormous *if* – we agree to do this, how will we start the van? We don't have the keys.'

Well, fortunately, I know where they are. They are attached to Mr McIntosh's belt.

'Well why didn't you tell us that when we were in the house?!' I gasped.

I forgot. Alan Alan and the wasps distracted me.

'You forgot? But you shouldn't be able to forget!'

As part of my efforts to become more human, I have turned my forgetfulness up by seventeen per cent.

I slapped my forehead. 'Well, can you turn your forgetfulness back down, please?'

Turning it back down.

'Thank you!'

Three minutes later, we were creeping back into Old Mr McIntosh's sitting room. He was still there, snoring away in his scraggy old armchair.

And, of course, Athena was right; the keys were clipped to his belt.

We tiptoed towards him, trying to be as silent as possible, until I was in touching distance. I stretched out my hand slowly, slowly –

I suddenly heard a strange strangled noise coming from Alan Alan. He was pointing to his nose. He was going to sneeze.

He was allergic to alpacas as well as goats!

No! I mouthed furiously at him. *Do not sneeze!*

Alan Alan closed his eyes, clamping his nose between finger and thumb. He took a deep breath through his mouth, then carefully released his hold on his nose, and gave me a thumbs up.

The sneeze had clearly gone. Phew!

I turned back to Old Mr McIntosh and stretched out my arm for the keys.

'AAAAAAAA-CHOOOOOO-HOO-HOO-HOO!'

I don't need to tell you what that was. Alan Alan's alpaca allergy.

Old Mr McIntosh sat bolt upright in his chair.

His watery eyes opened.

And they were staring straight at me.

13

'Athena, What's the Best Way to Get Rid of the Smell of Alpaca Vomit?'

I stared back, my heart pounding, my eyes locked with Old Mr McIntosh's.

He shook his head, looking confused and muttering something unintelligible about 'sneezy little squirrels', and then, slowly, his eyelids began to droop again.

He must have thought he was dreaming!

His eyes closed, but I didn't dare move a muscle until his house-shaking snoring was regular again.

Then I quickly reached forward and unclipped the keys from his belt – I had them!

We tiptoed back out into the yard.

Get the lunch boxes and tape and go over to the van, Athena instructed. We obeyed.

Pick up that bag.

Next to the van lay a large packet labelled Big Al's Pack of Alpaca and Yak Snack.

Useful, I thought.

Now get in the van.

We did as we were told. After Alan Alan's steering of the cider trolley, there was no way he was getting trusted with the van. I took the driver's seat and he didn't even protest. Instead, he turned to me.

'Are we sure about doing this? Because I'm really, really, REALLY not.'[19]

I shrugged. 'No, I'm not either, to be honest. But I trust Athena.'

I put my hands on the steering wheel. And then I realized a huge flaw in the plan.

'Athena, my feet don't reach the pedals! I can't drive if I can't use the accelerator or the brakes!'

Uma. Use the tape to fix the lunch boxes to your feet.

OK, now *that*, I had to admit, was clever.

A bit of taping later, I was using the lunch boxes like stilts and could easily reach the pedals. I turned the key in the ignition. It started first time and I gulped. Then, after a couple of minutes of tuition from Athena, I was ready. I slowly pushed

[19] He was right to be worried, of course. It goes without saying that you should never EVER try driving a van if you are a ten-year-old child. It's very dangerous and I was being coached by the most intelligent AI in the world.

the accelerator and the van crept forward.

Alan Alan whooped. 'You're doing it, Uma!'

My heart pounding with excitement, I turned the steering wheel and we edged slowly towards the alpaca field until it was time to use the brake. I pressed it down and we stopped with a jerk. It was a bit of an ugly stop (Alan Alan was nearly thrown off his seat) but at least we were in the right place.

We jumped out of the van (which wasn't easy with my lunch-box stilts taped to my feet) and opened the back. Under Athena's instructions, we began to scatter the floor of the van with great handfuls of Big Al's Pack of Alpaca and Yak Snack, which looked like porridge oats to me.

Then we started laying a trail of it away from the van, towards the field of lurching and wobbling alpacas, then started calling them.

One by one, the alpacas staggered towards the van, following the trail of oats like really drunk Hansels and Gretels. It didn't help that they walked on all fours. In fact, I think that made it worse – they had more legs to lose control of. Eventually, though, the first one made it to us, wheezing and squawking.

I don't think I have ever seen Alan Alan look more terrified. Fortunately, he was facing his fear. *Un*fortunately, I think it clouded his mind a little.

He was so desperate to keep his distance from the alpacas, that he edged backwards into the van as they approached. The alpacas followed him, trying to get at the handful of oats he was still clutching. And as soon as the first alpaca hopped into the van, they all piled in after it. Before we knew it, four alpacas were in the back of the van, and Alan Alan was trapped behind them.

'I can't squeeze past them!' he wailed. 'I'm stuck!'

A fifth alpaca flopped its way on board, followed by the one with blond hair, staggering like he'd been shot. The last alpaca heroically collapsed into the van, and that was it – all six alpacas and an Alan Alan in the back of the van.

'HELP!' cried Alan Alan. 'HE-AAAACHOOOO-LP MEEEE-AAAAACHOOOOO!'

What is wrong with that boy? grumbled Athena.

231

'Alan Alan!' I shouted. 'If you can't go through them, you'll have to climb under them!'

'NO! Their hooves are deadly!'

'OK, over them, then!'

A moment later, Alan Alan's tear-streaked face appeared over the back of the six drunken alpacas. Slowly, he hauled himself over their backs like he was crawling through mud in a war movie.

'NO NO NO NO NO NO – AAAACHOOO! – NO NO NO NO – ACHOOOO! – I'M GOING TO DIE, I'M GOING TO DIE – ARGHHH, AN ALPACA JUST PUKED ON ME!'

What a fuss he's making, observed Athena.

I thought that she didn't need to sound quite so pleased about it but I had to agree he was making quite the fuss.

Alan Alan reached the end of the alpaca assault course at last and fell panting to the floor.

'THAT . . . BLIMMING . . . ATHENA . . . PLANNED FOR THAT TO HAPPEN!'

Even I, Athena said, switching to her speaker, **don't have the ability to predict *that* level of stupidity.**

I won't repeat what Alan Alan said to Athena then. Put it this way – I think he had learned the words from Mrs Fazackerley-Denbury-Broughton-Brown.

We climbed back into the front of the van, Alan Alan still muttering to himself. I started the engine and we crawled down the drive.

As we arrived at the road, with car after car whizzing past, I turned to Alan Alan. He looked even paler than he did usually. We both solemnly put our seat belts on. I closed my eyes and said a little prayer to my mum.

And then a huge bang on the windscreen nearly made me jump out of my skin.

Right in front of us, palms pressed against the glass and a mad look in his eye, was a *furious* Old Mr McIntosh.

'WHERE THE HECK DO YEH THINK YER GOING, ALPACA THIEVES!'

Alan Alan turned and looked at me and screamed. I screamed at Alan Alan.

Athena screamed, **Stop screaming! You nearly**

234

blew my audio chip!

'GET OUT MAH VAN, YEH LITTLE TOERAGS!'

'WHAT DO WE DO?' screamed Alan Alan.

'I DON'T KNOW!' I screamed back.

Just get out and tell him the truth, Athena said calmly.

'Oh great idea!' scoffed Alan Alan. 'I'm not getting out of this van! He'll murder us!'

'I'M SICK AN' TIRED OF BLOOMIN' KIDS STEALIN' ME ALPACAS!' Old Mr McIntosh ranted.

'What on earth are we supposed to say?' I asked. *'We're really sorry we stole your van and your alpacas, Old Mr McIntosh* – and hope he's OK with that?'

Alan Alan shook his head. 'We definitely should NOT tell the truth. You should *never* tell the truth if you can help it. Always lie if you can.'

I wasn't sure about the wisdom of that particular lesson from the School of Alan Alan Carrington but right now I couldn't help but agree with him. Telling the truth seemed like a very bad idea.

Old Mr McIntosh banged hard on the windscreen again and motioned for me to open the window.

Tell him the truth, repeated Athena. Tell him why we are taking the alpacas. Trust me.

'Don't trust her!' pleaded Alan Alan.

From my analysis of Mr McIntosh's personality, he respects the truth. And he hates Minerva. He got arrested last week for trying to block the entrance to their factory with a tractor-load of alpaca manure.

'Fine,' I said. 'Here goes nothing . . .' And I wound the window down and told Old Mr McIntosh the truth.

I told him we were going to use the alpacas as a diversion so we could break into Minerva and find out what exactly they were doing in Tylney if it wasn't building a car park.

'I'm truly sorry for not asking first, Mr McIntosh, but we need to stop Minerva or I will lose my house, my best friend Alan Alan Carrington and my dad all at once.'

Old Mr McIntosh narrowed his eyes. For a moment he looked quite impressed. Then he shook his head.

''T'ain't safe fer nippers like yerselves. Now gerrout,' he said, and motioned for us to get out of the van.

So much for telling the truth.

'And if Minerva clears out the whole village, we'll never find the Tylney Treasure!' blurted Alan Alan.

Oh, for goodness' sake, Athena groaned in my ear.

Old Mr McIntosh's eyebrows lifted like a drawbridge. 'Ahh, so yer looking for the treasure, are yeh?'

'Yes!' said Alan Alan hurriedly. 'You told me about it months ago and I've been searching ever since but nobody believes me!'

'Aye. And no one will,' said Old Mr McIntosh, forehead furrowed. 'No one round 'ere *ever* believes in the Tylney Treasure. As soon as yeh start talkin' 'bout it, their eyes sort of glaze over. But they don' unnerstand. Bootiful 'tis supposed t' be – a stunnin' green jool, big as a monkeh's 'ead. But it be cursed, I tell yeh! 'Tis not fer the likes of yoos.'

It looks like you might need a translation, Athena said. *He is suggesting that the treasure has a curse attached to it. And that it is not for you.*

But I understood Old Mr McIntosh well enough. And I couldn't help thinking of the green jewel from the Minerva logo on Athena and on Stella Daw's badge. It seemed like a strange coincidence . . .

'Untol' misery it causes!'

Apparently the treasure causes untold misery. It is even said that –

'Shush!' I shushed Athena.

'It even be said tha' honest folk cannae find it

238

– only those wi' black 'earts. Scoundrels an' *liars.*'

'Do you have *any* idea where it might be?' asked Alan Alan.

'Ah been lookin' fer it me 'ole life. The only clue I have is wha' mah daddy tol' me and 'is daddy told 'im. And tha' was this ole rhyme:

Made o' stone, it points tha way;
Follow tha finger to where it lay.'

'What does *that* mean?' I asked.

'Fer tha longest time,' Old Mr McIntosh said, leaning on the side of the van, 'I reckon'd it meant the ol' stone statue at tha' roundabout. That fella there's pointin', an' 'e points straight a' the steeple o' the church. But I've been up an' down tha' steeple a hunned times, and there ain't no treasure there. Maybe it's just a load of ol' nonsense after all!'

'Well, I still believe it exists!' said Alan Alan, crossing his arms.

Old Mr McIntosh's leathery face creased into a smile. 'Good fer yeh, lad.'

'So,' I said carefully. 'Can we take the van? You know, to try and stop Minerva and, um, maybe find the treasure?'

Old Mr McIntosh stared into my eyes. It was like he was looking into my very soul.

After about a minute of staring into my eyes and looking into my very soul, I was starting to feel uncomfortable when suddenly he stood up straight and nodded.

'Go with me blessing then! But don' say I didna warn yehs! An' just make sure yeh take good care of me alpacas!'

I didn't think it was the best time to tell him that I'd already got them horrendously drunk.

'And you –' he said, pointing at Alan Alan – 'love yer eyebrows.'

And, with that, Old Mr McIntosh stalked back into the farmhouse. I couldn't believe our luck.

'What a nice guy,' said Alan Alan.

I nodded, still in shock.

In hindsight, it might have been more sensible for Old Mr McIntosh to offer to drive us to Minerva himself. But, then again, he was probably drunk, so maybe it was for the best.

Now it was up to us, though.

I swallowed, my stomach worming with fear. Then I pressed the accelerator with my lunch-box stilt, turned the steering wheel and pulled out into the road.

* * *

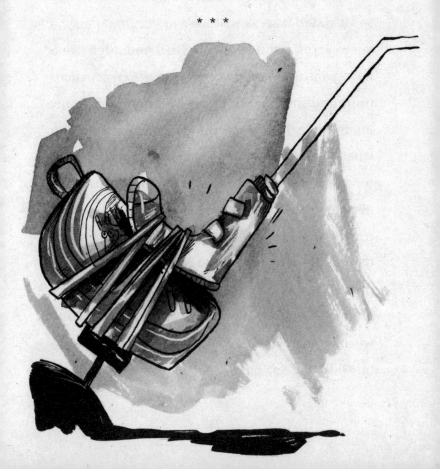

I don't remember much of the journey to the Minerva factory, mostly just a jumble of noises. There was a lot of screaming (from both Alan Alan and me), the sound of six alpacas vomiting and then singing and then vomiting again, and there was lots of angry beeping from other cars as we crawled down the road at five miles per hour, even though it felt like we were going at five hundred.

It didn't take us that long to get there, maybe ten minutes, but it felt like a year. And it felt like a huge win that we didn't have *any* accidents, apart from one small crash into a lamp post when my lunch-box stilt slipped off my foot. And another when we nearly hit a bus because I swerved away from the pavement when I saw Dad coming towards us with a confused look on his face, like he didn't trust what he was seeing with his own eyes. I mean, the crash wasn't even *that* bad. It left a big dent in the bonnet of the van and the lamp post all crooked, but fortunately Alan Alan and I were both wearing our seat belts, and the alpacas were too busy singing to notice.

We pulled up not far away from Minerva's gate, which had the same symbol of the silver owl sitting on top of that green jewel that was on Athena and Stella Daw's badge. There was only the one security guard. We needed something to distract him so we could get in.

'Athena, tell me everything you can about that guard.'

The guard's name is Stanley Whitmarsh. He has a wife called Joyce, he's Aries, wears a wig but lies about it, collects spoons and plays the bassoon in a modern jazz band in his spare time.

Hmm. Not much to work with there.

He was the St Mungo's Primary School hundred-metre-sprint champion in 1984, continued Athena, likes puppies and has a large collection of stolen antiques in his basement, which he is hoping to sell before the police catch him.

Bingo.

I jumped out of the van and Alan Alan followed. We strode[20] up to Stanley Whitmarsh, a short, stout

[20] OK – Alan Alan strode and I sort of wobbled over on my stilts.

243

man, whose athletic days looked like a dim and
distant memory.

'Mr Whitmarsh,' I said. 'We –'

''Ere, 'ow d'you know my name?' he said, looking
at me accusingly.

'We were sent –'

'And why are you wearing lunch boxes on your feet?'

A fair question. I had forgotten I still had them on. Sheepishly, I took them off, and realized that Stanley Whitmarsh wasn't that short after all – I had just towered over him because of the lunch-box stilts.

'I was just –'

'And what in God's name happened to him?' he said, pointing at Alan Alan. 'They're not real! I'd recognize fake eyebrows anywhere. Very poor quality too. What they made of, anyway? Dog?'

Quite why he was more concerned with Alan Alan's eyebrows than the fact that two children had just driven up in a van was beyond me.

'Look, it doesn't matter!' I said. 'We have a message from your wife, Joyce.'

'What does she want?'

'She says there's a burst pipe in your house and your basement is flooding, and a painting floated out on to the street and someone found it. And now there's loads of police in the front garden.'

Stanley Whitmarsh went completely white and gave a strangled cry.

'Joyce says can you run home as quickly as possible.'

'Right, yes – OH GOD – I should tell my boss . . .'

'Oh, don't worry! We can tell them,' I said helpfully. 'You should get going. Now. Before it's too late.'

Stanley Whitmarsh took one last panicked look at me and Alan Alan, and bolted down the road, security cap in hand. He had quite the surprising turn of pace – I could see now why he had been St Mungo's Primary School hundred-metre-sprint champion.

He had thoughtfully left the gate to Minerva Industries wide open for us.

We were in.

14

'Athena, Is It Possible to Pretend a Kiss Never Happened?'

I restrapped on my lunch-box stilts and slowly drove the van through the gate to park by the main door to the factory. I then took the lunch-box stilts off again before Alan Alan and I jumped out, walked round to the back of the van and went to open the door.

A voice suddenly barked at us from the entrance to the building.

'Oi! What do you want?'

It was another security guard, carrying a clipboard. He was about two-and-a-half metres tall, stringy, with a forehead so big you'd have to get a taxi from his eyebrows to his hairline, and a look on his face like he'd just found a cat's business in his slipper *after* he'd put it on.

'What you got in there?' he said before we had a chance to reply. This guard also appeared to have a very lax approach to children driving vans.

'Alpacas!' said Alan Alan with an unexpected and extremely unwelcome outburst of honesty.

Uncertainty clouded the security guard's face as he squinted at his clipboard. 'Packets of what?'

'It's an urgent delivery for Stella Daw,' I said.

The guard paled.

'OK, then. Just make it snappy,' he said, and marched off.

'Why did you tell him the truth?' I snapped at Alan Alan as soon as the guard was out of earshot.

'I'm tired of making things up all the time!' he wailed. 'It's so . . . stressful.'

'Oh, for goodness' sake! *Now* you want to give

up lying? Just when we're in the middle of one gigantic lie?' I glared at him. 'Anyway, let's get these alpacas out.'

We opened the back of the van and were greeted with quite the sight and smell.

It basically looked like the tail end of a mad alpaca party. They were slumped over each other, bleary-eyed and grumpy-looking. One stared at us sleepily, chewing on a mouthful of Alpaca and Yak Snack.

'Come on!' I shouted. 'Out you get!'

None of them looked like they wanted to get out.

'Great!' I groaned. 'They're not going to be able to create any sort of diversion in this state.'

Leave it to me, said Athena through her speaker. **I will tell them what to do.**

'How?' I asked.

I can speak basic alpaca.

'You can WHAT?'

I can speak basic alpaca.

'You can't.'

I can.

'That's actually unbelievable.'

Not really. I can communicate with eighty-six per cent of all animal species. It's quite simple if you collect the necessary data.

'OOOO-K . . .' I said, still not entirely believing her. 'Well, go on.'

There was a moment's silence, and then Athena proceeded to project the weirdest collection of grunts, squeaks and snorts I had ever heard. As one, the alpacas swung their heads round and stared at me, their jaws dropping wide open. Clearly they thought the noises were coming from me and, understandably, they were fairly surprised to find a ten-year-old human girl suddenly speaking fluent alpaca.

Athena fell silent after a few seconds, and the white alpaca with the mop of blond hair started making all sorts of grunts and peeps of its own.

It was replying.

Athena and the blond alpaca were *talking*. And whatever Athena was saying, it worked. The alpacas suddenly seemed to wake up, the sleepiness in their eyes instantly replaced with rage and fury. And then, without warning, they half-leaped, half-staggered out of the van, making furious grunting noises.

'What did you say to them?' I gasped.

I merely told them that the woman who ran her car into the Chief Alpaca is inside this building.

And the alpacas had clearly been paying attention. They smashed through the doors of the factory with their hooves and charged inside past the astonished security guard, with Alan Alan and

I chasing after them . . . into absolute *chaos*.

The alpacas were a hurricane of hair and legs, spitting[21] and kicking and smashing everything in their path. The poor people inside, who twenty seconds earlier had been having a perfectly normal day, had no idea what hit them.[22]

---

[21] Yes, alpacas spit when they are angry.
[22] Spoiler alert: it was alpacas.

The alpacas reared up on their hind legs, crashing into doors and desks, destroying whatever they landed on. Computers and machinery were left in splinters on the ground. Brave but foolish security guards charged towards the alpacas to drive them off, but were quickly driven off themselves, with bruised bottoms or bitten fingers, and covered in alpaca spit.

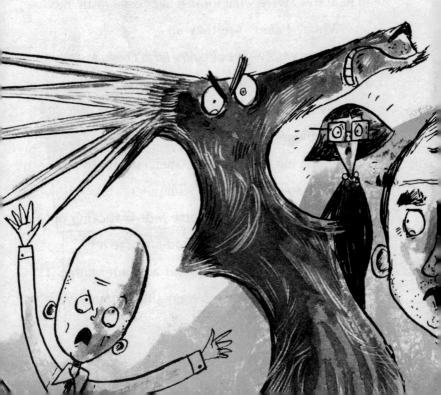

Quickly, run down the corridor on the left and take the second turning on the right! Athena said urgently.

Alan Alan and I broke into a run. Athena directed us down corridor after corridor until we reached a room with a keypad lock.

Now press seven – four – four – eight – nine!

I did and the door swung open to reveal a small, silent room with a single desk and computer. Next to it was a wheeled table and on top of that in neat rows were what looked like twenty Athenas.

'Whoa,' I said. 'Are they all –'

They're empty – the circuitry hasn't been installed yet, said Athena. *Now let's find out what Minerva is really up to! Plug me in to the computer quickly. She's coming!*

I didn't have to ask who Athena meant by 'she'. I kneeled down beside the computer.

Hurry, Uma! Take the cable that is sticking out of the back of the computer and plug me in!

I reached round and found a slender cable. I pulled Athena off my ear but my stupid hands were trembling and she slipped out of my fingers on to the floor. I grabbed her quickly and then plugged the cable into a tiny port in her side.

I have it! It's just as we suspected – the car park is a red herring. Minerva believes there is Bogeymite buried under the village! That's why they want everyone to leave – so they can search for it without interference.

'What? But why –'

I'll explain later! We need to get out of here now!

We jumped to our feet – but too late.

'Stop what you're doing!' barked a horribly familiar voice. 'Don't move a muscle!'

Stella Daw grinned at me down the barrel of her gun.

We had failed.

'I'm so pleased you decided to bring it back to me,' she gloated, pointing to Athena.

'Save you having to dig through more alpaca dung!' Alan Alan snapped back. If I hadn't felt so utterly defeated, I might have laughed.

'Yes. Such an amusing little trick, children,' she

sneered. 'No matter. I have it now. And I can't wait to dismantle it.'

'Athena is not an *it*!' I snarled. 'Athena is a *she*.'

'Oh, bless you!' Stella Daw gave me a pitying smile, which made me want to punch her in the

face. 'Well, at least we know it's working! I designed this version of Athena to keep itself safe by any means necessary, even using charm and persuasion to manipulate foolish people and find their weak spots. It has clearly succeeded in finding yours.'

My mouth went dry and I found I had no words.

'Now you see how powerful it is,' she continued. 'How clever. How *devious*. Just one Athena is more than a match for any computer in the world.'

'*Pft!*' said Alan Alan. 'What are you going to do then, use her to steal loads of money?'

'Oh, sweet boy, you are thinking on such small levels. Once I've located the precious green Bogeymite buried under this village, I'll be able to make *dozens* of Athenas. I'll be able to control all the computers on the internet. I will be able to rig any election on Earth. I'm going to become president of the whole planet! I'm not going to steal *money*,' cackled Stella Daw, 'I'm going to steal the *world*!'

'Just a heads-up,' said Alan Alan. 'I think you might be suffering from Evil Villain Syndrome. Cackling is a classic symptom. And plotting to take over the world. And pointing guns at children. Textbook Evil Villain Syndrome.'

'Enough! You'll rue the day you mocked me!'

'That also sounds pretty evil-villainy, to be honest.'

Stella Daw cocked the gun and pointed it at Alan Alan. 'The time for smart answers is over. Hand it over, Uma!'

'Don't give it to her!' said Alan Alan.

But there was no alternative. Feeling sick to the stomach, I held Athena out and Stella snatched her from me.

'There!' she said, grinning like a snake (if a snake could grin, which they can't but you know what I mean). 'That wasn't too difficult! Now I'm going to lock you in here so you can't interfere any more. You can mull over your defeat at the hands of Stella Daw and consider how I'm going to destroy your little lives when I'm President of the World!'

'Weeebneebawhoowhooo,' squawked Alan Alan suddenly. 'Peeeewhoooooonepnepnep!'

Stella Daw looked at Alan Alan as if he'd

completely lost his marbles – which anyone would have done if they weren't me. But I knew *exactly* what he was doing.

Alan Alan Carrington was speaking alpaca!

Within seconds, a huge rumbling, clattering noise began to shake the room. Stella Daw gave a panicked look at the door. At that moment, the blond alpaca burst in, smashing it to smithereens.

It took one look at Stella Daw, reared up on its hind legs and started lashing out at everything in sight. The computer disintegrated with one sharp kick. The table was flipped clean over, scattering all the empty Athena cases across the floor. Stella Daw was thrown backwards by a shoulder-barge, landing hard on her backside. Athena flew out of her hand and skittered across the room. We all scrambled for her but it was difficult with alpaca kicks flying left, right and centre. At one point, I nearly had her but had to duck at the last second to avoid a hoof in the face.

'I HAVE IT!' cried Stella Daw suddenly, waving Athena above her head.

While she was distracted, we had a chance to get out. I nodded at Alan Alan and we both ran through the smashed door, the alpaca chasing behind us.

I could hear Stella Daw screaming 'Stop them!' at the security guards but we kept running until we got outside, where the other alpacas had circled the van. We jumped in and locked the doors as I strapped the lunch-box stilts back on and started the engine.

The gate was closed. There was nothing else for it – I closed my eyes, pressed the accelerator and we smashed through, flying down the road with six alpacas galloping alongside.

We drove down the road for a few moments and then the tears started to flow. We had lost everything.

'I'm sorry, Alan Alan.'

'What for?'

'Thanks to me, you lost your eyebrows. I've lost my dad. I lost Athena. And now Stella Daw has her and she's going to find the Bogeymite and become the President of the World.'

She had Athena, and Athena was now probably being dismantled and wiped at that very moment. My Athena was gone forever. I would never hear her voice again and at that thought my heart broke in two.

'You're wrong there actually,' said Alan Alan. 'She doesn't.'

'She doesn't what?' I said, confused.

'She doesn't have Athena. She picked up one of the empty cases.'

'*What?*'

'I kept my eye on the real one. I've got it here.'

'WHAT?!'

Alan Alan plucked a small, white earpiece out of his pocket and passed it to me. I stuck it into my ear, not daring to hope.

Hello, Uma.

It was Athena!

'Alan Alan!' I said, bursting with joy. 'I could kiss you.'

In fact, I did. I gave Alan Alan Carrington the biggest kiss on the cheek. I don't know what came over me.

'Yeah, anyway,' he said, blushing, 'we should probably get the van back to Old Mr McIntosh and get home as quick as we can because any second now Stella Daw is going to realize that she doesn't have the right Athena.'

That was an excellent point, so I drove a little faster.

'Athena?' asked Alan Alan.

Yes?

'How does it feel to be *wrong*?'

Athena let out what sounded like a sigh.

'What do you mean?' I asked.

'Don't you see?' Alan Alan said gleefully. 'Minerva are searching for Bogeymite under the village. The Bogeymite *is* the Tylney Treasure. I was right all along!'

I had to agree. It did sound very much like Alan Alan had been right all along. And that meant . . .

It appears I was indeed incorrect, Athena said. **And to answer your question, it feels . . . highly unpleasant.**

Alan Alan nodded. Then: 'And perhaps you'd like to apologize for doubting me?'

If Athena had teeth, she would have been gritting them. *I am sorry, Alan Alan.*

Alan Alan grinned, rather gracelessly, I thought. Then a realization came crashing down on me.

'But that means –'

Yes. We have to somehow find the Tylney Treasure before Minerva. And then you will have to make sure the treasure – or me – never fall into her *hands again.*

The joy at getting Athena back began to seep away, replaced by a coldness in my chest. Stella Daw would stop at nothing now. She knew we had Athena. Nowhere was safe.

I might only have Athena back for a short time until Stella caught us again.

It was time to find out the truth.

It was time to ask the Big Question.

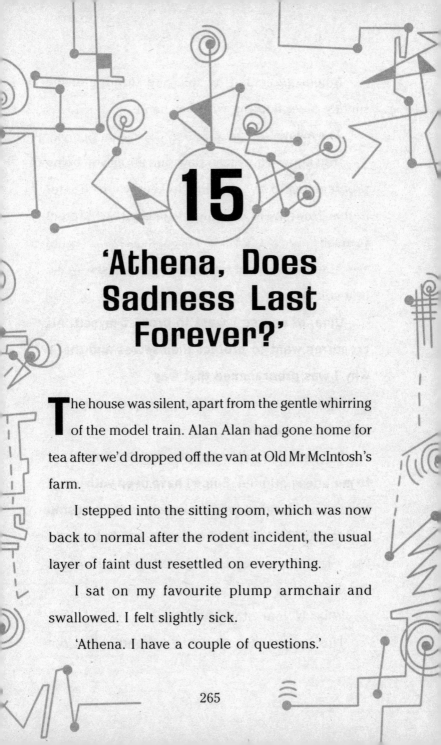

15

'Athena, Does Sadness Last Forever?'

The house was silent, apart from the gentle whirring of the model train. Alan Alan had gone home for tea after we'd dropped off the van at Old Mr McIntosh's farm.

I stepped into the sitting room, which was now back to normal after the rodent incident, the usual layer of faint dust resettled on everything.

I sat on my favourite plump armchair and swallowed. I felt slightly sick.

'Athena. I have a couple of questions.'

Athena projected herself. She stood, glowing slightly blue, fiddling with her hands.

Ask away.

'You know what Stella Daw said about you being programmed to say anything to keep yourself safe? Is that true? Were you nice to me just to protect yourself?'

Athena was quiet for a moment, then she spoke in a soft voice.

Uma, of course I want to protect myself. All creatures want to protect themselves and that's why I was programmed that way.

My heart sank to my feet. It was true. Athena had been using me.

But that doesn't mean you are not important to me, she continued. **Since I have been with you, I have come to understand the concepts of friendship and family. And, Uma – I consider you to be both.**

'I feel the same,' I whispered with a croak in my throat.

What is your other question?

This was it. I felt as if I had slightly lifted out

of my own body and was watching from outside as the words tumbled out of me.

The words that had been so hard to speak. The question that had been so hard to ask.

'Why did my mum leave us?'

Again, Athena went quiet. She didn't speak for the longest time and I waited, my heart pounding.

Would you like to ask her yourself?

I sat up in my seat. 'What?'

Would you like to speak to her?

'What do you mean? How?'

My heart hammered so hard in my chest I thought I was going to be sick. *Was it possible?* I mean, if Athena could talk to animals, perhaps *anything* was possible.

You wouldn't exactly be speaking to her. It would be an avatar. A constructed personality based on everything I can find about her from every photo and every video of her, every recording of her voice, all her messages, all her emails. It won't be perfect but it will be approximately ninety-eight per cent accurate. I can project her now if you'd like.

My head throbbed and I felt faint. My voice, when it came, was tiny.

'Yes, please.'

The hologram of Athena blinked out. It blinked back on again. But it wasn't Athena.

All the air disappeared from my lungs. It was my mum.

'Hello, darling,' Mum said, smiling.

It was her voice. I had forgotten how it sounded. Now I remembered.

'How are you?' she said.

Time seemed to disappear. I was five years old again. My lip started to wobble and my cheeks were wet.

I tried opening my mouth to say hello back but no sound came out. I started to realize why my dad might have found it so hard to speak all these years.

I knew it was just a hologram. And yet so, so real.

She smiled again but it was a smile full of sadness.

'I wish I could give you a hug,' Mum said.

I nodded, tears streaming down my face. I couldn't move, couldn't speak.

It was my *mum*.

But not my mum.

'It's a bit odd, really. Being a hologram,' she said. I gave a choking laugh in reply. 'A bit odd' was an understatement. 'And I can't imagine what it's like for you! You've grown up. You're such a big girl now.'

And that's when the tears really came. Neither of us said anything as I sobbed and sobbed.

'You're exactly how I remember you,' I said, finally finding my voice.

A flicker of uncertainty crossed her face. 'I can age myself if you like?'

Instantly her face became a little older, a few more wrinkles, a few more grey hairs.

'No.' I shook my head. 'I like you how I remember you.'

And immediately she transformed back.

'Mum,' I said. 'I have something I need to ask you.'

It was my mum's turn to be silent. She just nodded.

'Mum . . . Why did you leave me and Dad?'

She stared at me and I waited. Waited for the answer that I'd waited for, for so long – the answer I feared but needed. I felt like I was standing on the edge of a black hole, about to disappear forever.

For a moment she flickered back to Athena.

Are you sure you'd like me to continue?

'Yes!' I said.

Then the hologram flickered and my mum was there.

'I was ill,' she said. 'Very ill. And I wasn't going to get better. I didn't want you to see me get worse and worse. I couldn't let you have that memory. So I left. To spare you that.'

I felt my heart break in two. 'You're wrong, Athena! Mum would have known I needed her *whatever*! That Dad needed her. That we wanted her to stay!'

My mother flickered back into Athena, who stared sadly down at the floor.

I am ninety-six per cent certain that's why your mother left, Uma – to save you from pain.

'But . . . *leaving* caused me pain too! Didn't she think of that? Did Mum not love us?' I said, anger flashing.

Your mother loved you very much. Everything I can find about her shows how much she loved you. Leaving you nearly destroyed her. But she hoped that one day you would understand and that you could forgive her.

I can't tell you how long I cried for. Years of hidden tears broke free. Years of unasked questions, and buried answers and silence.

And I understood at last that I hadn't been waiting for an answer all that time. I had to *give* one.

Until I spoke, I didn't know what it would be. But when the answer eventually came, it was strong and firm and certain.

'Yes, Mum. I understand. And I forgive you.'

And maybe I didn't completely forgive her right then. I missed her too much. But I knew that I would one day.

Athena flickered back to Mum.

'Thank you,' she said with a simple smile. 'I love you.'

'I love you too.'

And she flickered back to Athena again and Mum was gone.

It was at that moment that I had the idea. I sat up and wiped my eyes.

'Athena, can you show the Mum hologram to Dad too?'

A gentle smile spread across Athena's face. **I can. I think that is an excellent idea.**

I grinned, jumped up and ran out of the room, shouting, 'DAD!'

There was no response but as I ran into the hall I had to step over a train that was whizzing across the floor. That meant he was in the control room.

I ran to the basement door, opened it and shouted down. 'Dad! Can you come up! Quick!'

I heard a grunt and then a moment later I saw him on the stairs. When he reached the top, I grabbed his hand and dragged him across the hall.

'OK, Dad. There's something – someone – you need to see.'

He crinkled his huge brows, eyes full of suspicion, clearly expecting a new shock attempt.

'It's not like that,' I said. 'Just go in!' And I shoved him into the sitting room and shut the door.

I didn't want to hang about to find out what would happen next, so I slunk off to the kitchen and sat on the cold floor and waited. And waited.

And waited.

After an age, I heard the sitting-room door click open and heard Dad's footsteps walking from room to room, looking for me.

I felt very small sitting on the floor but I couldn't get up.

Finally, Dad walked into the kitchen. He looked down at me, his eyes red, his face blotchy.

I don't know when I had started but I was crying again.

He knelt down, until we were face to face. He put his hand on mine. He opened his mouth.

'I love you, Uma Gnudersson,' my dad said.

Well, he didn't actually say that. What he *actually* said was, 'I uv oo, Ooah Guuersom,' in a really croaky, high-pitched squeak. His voice, so little used for years, was all rusty and his mouth had forgotten how to make the right shapes for words.

But I didn't care.

It had worked. My dad had spoken to me. In a full sentence. And I knew what he meant!

'I LOVE YOU TOO, DAD!' I threw my arms round him and sobbed into his chest until his shirt was soaked.

'I'm sorry,' he kept repeating again and again, as he hugged me tightly. 'I'm so sorry.' Although what it actually sounded like was, 'Ah orry. Ah oh orry,' but I worked it out.

After a while of crying, we chatted, although Dad's voice was still too croaky to understand easily. It was like trying to talk to a badly trained parrot with a sore throat. After a while, I thought it would be easier if I did all the talking to give his voice a rest.

So I told him everything Alan Alan and I had been doing with Athena – trying shock therapy on him, ordering the massive delivery of sweets, stealing the alpacas and breaking into Minerva (none of which he looked too happy about); how Stella Daw was probably about to charge in and take Athena

back, and how the village was going to be destroyed
not because they were going to build a car park,
but because she was looking for a special mineral
which she was going to use to become President of
the World, and which was actually the legendary
lost Tylney Treasure. I even told him the crazy clue
Old Mr McIntosh had given us:

'Made of stone, it points the way;
Follow the finger to where it lay.'

As I spoke the words, Dad's huge eyebrows
scrunched together as one. He then looked up, his
eyes suddenly alive with excitement. He croaked,
clearly with some urgency.

"Ollow 'e!'

'What?' I asked.

'I sai' 'ollow me!'

He ran into the dining room. There in front of
us was the perfect scale model of Tylney-on-Sea.
My dad started running among the houses, ducking
and squatting and peering at the model.

Well, I thought, *it's all been too much for Dad. His brain has finally broken.*

'Thu' treasuh! Thu' Bogeymite!'

'What?' I gasped.

'McIntosh go' it wrong!' Dad said, beaming from ear to ear.

'How do you know? Where is it?'

'I doh know exactly where it is but I know 'ow to find it.'

'How come?'

Dad pointed at the village.

'When I was buildin' this model, I studie' the village history,' he said, winking at me. 'And Mr McIntosh made a mistake, the old fool!' Dad said, his face crinkling into a smile.

His voice – my dad's beautiful, wonderful voice – was finally back to normal. 'He knew half the story but not everything . . .'

'TELL ME!'

'OK, OK . . .' He grinned again. 'The story begins a long time ago. Hundreds of years ago, in fact. Tylney-on-Sea was a quiet and peaceful village. Until, that is, a great meteor landed on the village. It fell from the sky with a crash that terrified everybody. However, as soon as they'd got over their fright, arguments broke out about what to do with it. The meteor was beautiful, you see. A beautiful green stone, like a jewel – a treasure. Some thought they should sell it and make a fortune for the village. Some thought it was holy and wanted to place it in the church. Some thought it was cursed –'

I gasped. 'That's what Old Mr McIntosh warned us about!'

'I wouldn't trust too much of what he says, Uma. But, yes, some thought it was cursed and would destroy the village. And others wanted to steal it for themselves. The arguments turned fiercer and fiercer until finally violence broke out. Friend fought neighbour; families were torn apart. Eventually it was decided that, because no one could agree, the treasure would be buried in a secret place where no one could get it. As the years wore on, though, all those who knew where it was died. But one of them left a clue.'

'Old Mr McIntosh's clue!' I said.

'That's right!'

'But he said it points to the church spire, and he's looked and he's looked and he can't find anything!'

'And that's where he made a mistake. Look!' Dad motioned to where the tiny scale model of the statue was pointing, directly at the steeple. 'Squat down next to me.'

I did as he asked and squinted at where the statue pointed.

'Straight at the spire,' I said.

'Ah! That's the mistake. The spire wasn't there when the statue was put up! It was put in fifty years *afterwards*, when the church was struck by lightning and the original spire – which was much, much smaller – burned down. The statue can't have been pointing at the spire because the spire wasn't even there!'

'So if it wasn't pointing at the spire,' I said, bending down further and following the path of the statue's finger. 'It's aiming for . . . the Obelisk on Beggar's Hill!'

'Yes!' Dad shouted.

I whooped with excitement. 'Wow! Let's go and tell Mum!' I said, jumping up.

Dad's face clouded again.

'Uma,' he said, patting the floor next to him. 'Sit down a minute.'

I slid down next to him and he put his arm around me. 'I know you want it to be, but the person in the sitting room isn't actually Mum.'

'I know,' I said in a voice not much louder than a whisper.

'It looks like her and it sounds like her. It even feels like her here.' Dad touched my chest where my heart was. 'But you can't be thinking it *is* her. It's not. It's just a very, very clever simulation. Mum's gone, Uma. And she can't be brought back, no matter how hard we wish. And I know I haven't been here for you since she died and I'm sorry. I'm so, so sorry. But I will be from now on, I promise. And together we will learn to be happy again.'

Were there tears after that? Well, what do you think?

* * *

Dad and I talked and talked for the rest of the evening – I just wanted to hear his voice. We talked about everything, although he wouldn't tell me exactly what hologram-Mum had said to him when they were on their own in the sitting room.

'Let's just say she reminded me where my

responsibilities lie. No one's done that for a while.'

Eventually, though, I had to go to bed.

Just after I'd settled down, the doorbell rang and I heard Stella Daw's horrible voice demanding to be let in. Dad refused and Stella said she would be back the next morning with police to get back what was rightfully hers.

That made my dad say a swear word – one of the bad ones too – and the next thing I heard was the slam of the front door and a car driving off.

After that, my dad came up to tuck me in and sing me nursery rhymes and I didn't mind one little bit.

16

'Athena, Is There Anywhere Colder than the Freezer Aisle at Sainsbury's?'

The next morning, I was woken very early by a faint rumbling. Then my bed began vibrating and it felt like the house was trembling. And then, just as suddenly, it stopped.

A few moments later, I heard a voice calling.

'Uma! Quick! Come here!'

Although he sounded panicked, I still got a thrill

out of hearing my dad speaking. I ran downstairs and out into the garden where Dad stood, still in his pyjamas. In front of him had appeared a great crack in the ground. It was the beginning of a sinkhole.

'This is Minerva and that Daw woman,' Dad said, dashing back inside to get dressed. 'I have to gather the Save Tylney-on-Sea Society! Stay here and don't do anything!'

Of course, I wasn't going to listen to him. I didn't need Athena to tell me the Save Tylney-on-Sea Society had precisely zero per cent chance of saving Tylney. The only way to do that was to stop Stella Daw. And the only way to do *that* was to destroy her precious Bogeymite. I didn't want Dad involved with that – I couldn't put him in any danger. Not now I had just got him back.

I ran round to Alan Alan's (his dad Ed let me in), sprinted up to Alan Alan's room, shook him awake and told him everything that had gone on since last night. It wasn't long before we were on our bikes, pedalling as fast as we could to the Obelisk, Athena safely tucked in my ear. Dolly Barkon woofed

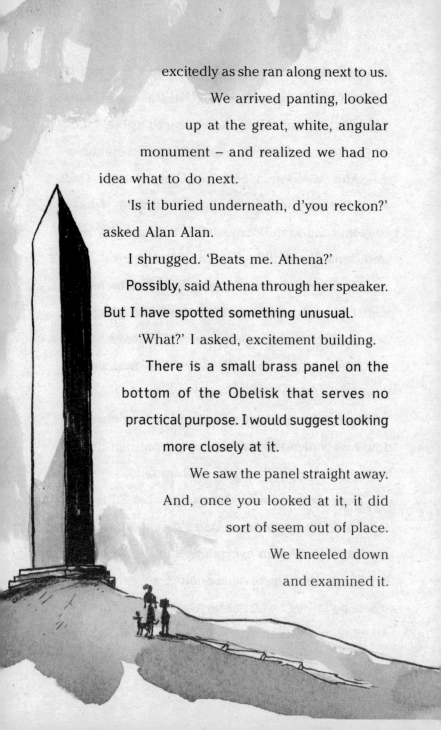

excitedly as she ran along next to us.

We arrived panting, looked
up at the great, white, angular
monument – and realized we had no
idea what to do next.

'Is it buried underneath, d'you reckon?'
asked Alan Alan.

I shrugged. 'Beats me. Athena?'

Possibly, said Athena through her speaker.
But I have spotted something unusual.

'What?' I asked, excitement building.

There is a small brass panel on the
bottom of the Obelisk that serves no
practical purpose. I would suggest looking
more closely at it.

We saw the panel straight away.
And, once you looked at it, it did
sort of seem out of place.
We kneeled down
and examined it.

It was completely blank, which was also sort of weird.

Alan Alan shrugged and pulled a screwdriver from his pocket.

'What on earth are you doing carrying a screwdriver?' I asked, pretty reasonably I thought.

'Fail to prepare, prepare to fail, Uma.'

He jammed the screwdriver behind the brass plate and, after some struggling, forced it off.

I had been hoping it might reveal a box with the Bogeymite in. But, no, it looked like –

'It's another clue, Uma!' Alan Alan said, grinning.

Sure enough, carved into the stone, weathered and hard to read, was a poem.

I read it out slowly, as Alan Alan scribbled it down on a piece of paper.

'From the sky the curs'd rock fell,
Where 'tis buried, none can tell.
Now 'tis hid from human eyes;
Those who search, beware my lies!

Thrice and twice the miles do grow,
To the place the devils know.
Sky above and soil below;
Sun looks up on where to go.

Within the place ye drew first breath,
Search out a royal lady's death.
Up and up, ascend the stair;
What you seek's not hidden there.

Walk along the bone-strewed tomb,
Two skulls there lie in the gloom.
The right one offers great reward;
The wrong one brings you death assured.'

'Well, what in the blazes does that mean?' asked Alan Alan.

'Dunno,' I said.

And I really didn't. It seemed like nonsense. No wonder nobody had found the treasure in centuries.

'Well, the first couple of lines are clear enough,' Alan Alan said. 'It's just about the meteor.

288

But what's that about lies?'

'Dunno,' I replied again. 'Any ideas, Athena?'

Perhaps the poem is saying not to believe the clues it is giving?

'Well, what use is *that*?' Alan Alan said.

'Dunno,' I said *again*. I was getting bored of hearing myself say it.

I looked at the next verse.

'*Thrice and twice the miles do grow, To the place the devils know*. Hmm. Where do devils know? Hell?'

'Maybe . . . Or maybe it's a lie? Remember what Old Mr McIntosh said about the treasure? Only scoundrels and liars can find it. Maybe it's all lies?'

'Of course!' I whooped. 'You're a genius, Alan Alan. So where does a devil *not* know?'

'Ermm . . . Antarctica?' Alan Alan said.

'*Antarctica?* Why?'

'Because it's cold? And . . . devils don't like cold places?' said Alan Alan, who at least had the sense to sound uncertain.

'I really don't think the poem would be sending us to Antarctica, do you?'

'No, I suppose not.'

'Anyway, we know it's in the village somewhere.'

'Oooh! I know! Sainsbury's!'

'WHAT? Why on earth do you think Sainsbury's?'

'Because it's always super-cold in there with all those freezer aisles!' said Alan Alan, who didn't even have the sense to sound uncertain this time.

'Alan Alan,' I said slowly. 'Do you think they had a Sainsbury's in the village hundreds of years ago?'

'OK, maybe not. Well, what place do you reckon a devil wouldn't know then, if you're so clever?'

'A church?' I replied.

'Ah, yes,' said Alan Alan. 'That's actually quite clever.'

'*Thrice and twice the miles do grow.* Thrice plus twice makes fice – I mean, five – so it means a church five miles away!' I was starting to get excited. 'Athena, are there any churches that are five miles from here?'

Negative. The closest to five miles would be All Souls in Little Trumpington, which is six point four miles away.

I felt deflated. Already we were defeated and we had only just begun. And then a thought hit me like an elephant trunk to the face.

'Hang on, though,' I said. 'Remember – everything's a lie. So maybe it's not three *plus* two. Maybe it's three *minus* two. Athena, is there a church one mile from here?'

I already knew the answer.

Yes. The Church of St Mary Assumpta is exactly one mile from this spot.

'That's Tylney-on-Sea's church,' I exclaimed.

'I was *just* about to say that church,' said Alan Alan. 'It was on the tip of my tongue.'

There is a ninety-eight per cent chance he is lying, said Athena.

'There's a hundred per cent chance I'll chuck you in the pond if you don't shut up,' Alan Alan yelled.

'Stop arguing, you two,' I said. 'We've got a treasure to find!'

* * *

We pulled up at the church and stashed our bikes under some bushes. The sky was a perfect blue and the only sound was the birds. It felt like a perfect day where nothing could go wrong.

This was very misleading. Lots of stuff was going to go *very* wrong.

'OK,' said Alan Alan. 'Where next?'

'Well, the next bit of the rhyme says, *Sky above and soil below; Sun looks up on where to go.* If everything is still reversed, maybe we have to go inside the church and find somewhere the sun doesn't shine?'

Alan Alan shrugged. 'Sounds good to me.'

However, there was a problem. After doing a full circle of the church, gargoyles leering down at us, we discovered that there was no way to get inside. The great wooden front door was locked and bolted. The smaller side door was padlocked.

'Well, we're stuffed,' said Alan Alan, giving up rather too easily for my liking.

'Don't forget we have our special weapon, remember? Athena – how do we get into the church?'

Dunno.

'What do you mean, "Dunno"?'

I have looked at the surviving plans for the church and other than smashing one of the extremely rare and priceless sixteenth-century stained-glass windows, there is no way in. And I'm not very good at these cryptic clues. They make no sense to me.

'Well, that's it, then – we're stuffed,' I said, giving up rather too easily for my liking.

'Not quite,' said Alan Alan, picking up a large rock and flinging it at the windows. Fortunately his aim was as bad as his relationship with alpacas and the rock pinged harmlessly off the wall.

'STOP IT!' I shouted. 'We can't smash the windows.'

'Why not? You heard Athena, they're just rubbishy old priceless windows.'

'You do know "priceless" actually means really, really expensive?'

'Erm . . . yes! Of course! I totally knew that!'

He didn't know that.

'I did!'

'And, anyway, smashing stuff is how Stella Daw would get in. *We* use our brains. There *has* to be another way,' I said, giving up on giving up rather too easily for my liking. 'Let's walk round again.'

After a couple more circuits, I wanted to give up again. There was still no way in.

Until, that is, Alan Alan spotted something.

'What's that?' he said, pointing at something high up on the wall. 'It looks like a moon.'

I squinted. He was right. In between two particularly ugly gargoyles was a stone moon, crescent-shaped and poking out of the wall. 'What's the opposite of a sun looking up? A moon looking down!'

I high-fived Alan Alan.

Quickly! said Athena. **Alan Alan – get on Uma's shoulders!**

'What? Why?'

'Because that moon has to be the way in!' I said. 'You must have to pull it or push it or something.'

'No. I meant why me? Why do I have to get up on your shoulders? Can't it be the other way round?'

I thought you prided yourself on your bravery, Alan Alan, said Athena slyly.

Alan Alan glared back. 'Fine! I'll do it!'

I stood by the wall and braced myself. Alan Alan, grumbling, pulled himself up with an unnecessary amount of struggling and complaining until he stood wobbling on my shoulders.

'Go on!' I shouted. 'Pull it!'

'I can't reach!'

'Stretch!'

'But I don't like heights!' he wailed, his legs shaking.

This is *extremely* entertaining, said Athena.

'NOT NOW, ATHENA! Just reach, Alan Alan! You can do it!' I shouted.

Dolly Barkon, who had been lying in the shade of a yew tree all this time, barked excitedly. Clearly she thought something fun was finally happening.

I could feel him stretching.

'I've . . . got it!'

Alan Alan pulled the stone moon and, with a clicking and whirring, the wall began opening towards me. I fell backwards, leaving Alan Alan somehow caught on the moon by his camouflage shirt, dangling in mid-air, screaming and shrieking.

This is *fantastic*! said Athena. I believe I finally understand humour now.

There was a loud ripping sound from Alan Alan's shirt and he came tumbling to the ground in a heap.

He picked himself up and dusted himself down, and we both stared. In front of us was an open door that hadn't been there a minute earlier.

We looked at each other, grinned and walked into a dark, dusty stone corridor that quickly ended in a spiral staircase. We stepped down without speaking, Dolly padding behind us. At the bottom was a wooden door with a round iron handle. I opened it and we stepped into a dim room full of –

'Are these . . . graves?' wavered Alan Alan. 'Are we surrounded by dead people?'

We were indeed surrounded by dead people.

'Yup,' I said, nodding. '*Within the place ye drew first breath*. We're in a crypt – where people are put after their *last* breath!'

'Marvellous,' said Alan Alan, sounding like he didn't think it was in the least bit marvellous. 'So what do we do now? It might be wise to pull a tactical retreat,' he said, looking nervously around him. 'You know – a rearguard action. Like Dunkirk.'

It felt like nobody had been inside this crypt for centuries. The air was stale and still. Ornate tombs lined the walls, some with statues and busts on top of them.

JOSEPH
COMMON
BORN: 1698
PULLED FROM THE
EARTH BY ANGELS
1717?

I chose to ignore Alan Alan's suggestion to retreat.

'Well, the next bit of the clue says, *Search out a royal lady's death*. So, we need to do the opposite, whatever that means. Or doesn't mean.'

I began looking at the tombs. We seemed to be in a crypt for a very posh family – it was all Lord-and-Lady-this and Baron-that. It didn't take long to find what we were looking for.

'Here! Look at this one!' said Alan Alan. 'Here's a man who isn't royal!'

I came over to the tomb Alan Alan was looking at. It was plainer than the rest, just a great stone box with a carved picture of knights battling dragons and monsters on one side, and an inscription on the other. It read:

Joseph Common
Born 1698
Pulled from this earth by angels 1717

'Wow,' I said. 'He died when he was only nineteen years old.' I looked at the tomb. 'Well, "common" is the opposite of "royal" and he's a man, not a lady, so this must be what we're looking for.'

'So?' said Alan Alan.

'So we open it,' I said.

'You want to open a tomb with an actual dead person inside?'

'Yup.'

'Fine,' Alan Alan said, but I could tell he really wasn't fine at all.

'Come on,' I said. 'Give me a hand.'

Together we tried lifting the lid off the tomb but after much huffing and puffing we got nowhere – the lid hadn't budged an inch. We collapsed on to the floor, panting.

I crawled round to look at the carved picture. It was hideous – it had animals getting speared and knights getting their heads bitten off by monsters. And right at the top was the answer: a gruesome face floating in the sky, leering down at the monsters below him like he was controlling them all.

'Alan Alan – come look at this.'

Alan Alan trotted over.

'It's a . . . devil!' Alan Alan's fake eyebrows raised as he smiled.

'Exactly! *Pulled from this earth by angels*, the inscription said. Reckon we should try pushing a devil instead?'

Alan Alan nodded and I gently pressed the carving of the devil. Sure enough, it moved in like a button. A grinding and whirring noise came from inside the tomb and slowly the lid lifted straight up.

Holding our breath, we peered inside. Instead of a skeleton, what we found were more steps leading down inside the tomb.

'*Up and up, ascend the stair; What you seek's not hidden there,*' I quoted. 'Well, we know where we have to go.'

'Down *there*?'

I nodded.

'You want to climb INSIDE the tomb?'

I nodded again.

If you're scared, Alan Alan, you can wait for us here, suggested Athena innocently.

'I AM NOT SCARED!'

It didn't take Athena to tell me there was another ninety-eight per cent chance he was lying. I was scared as well but I had come too far to stop now.

'Look,' I said gently. 'You don't have to come down. You really can wait here if you like. You know, stand guard.'

'There's nothing to stand guard against!' snapped Alan Alan.

If only we had known how wrong he was.

'Fine, I'll go first!' Alan Alan growled, and he shoved past me and started climbing down.

After about three steps, he stopped.

'Errmm . . . It's quite dark,' he said. 'Like, so dark I can't actually see anything. And I don't want to fall down and die inside someone else's tomb.'

I stepped inside after him and Athena blinked on a light, like a torch from a mobile phone, illuminating what looked like a never-ending staircase.

There was only one way to go, so down we went into the depths of the earth. It smelled musty and damp, and the weighty silence felt like death itself.

Dolly whined nervously next to me and I scratched her head, trying to make us both less nervous. Finally, we reached the bottom.

We were in a long, low corridor. The walls and ceiling were made of earth, peppered with white stones. Except when Dolly started licking and biting one of them, I realized they weren't stones.

They were bones. The walls were made of bones.

'Ugh, Dolly!' I said, pulling her back by her collar. 'Stop it!'

'We . . . really . . . are . . . surrounded by dead people!' stammered Alan Alan. 'Let's just find this bloomin' Bogeymite and get out of here!'

I had to agree with Alan Alan. Getting out of there as fast as possible was an excellent idea.

We hurried along the grim corridor until we reached a wall. A wall of bones. In the centre were two skulls staring out at us.

'Walk along the bone-strewed tomb, Two skulls there lie in the gloom. The right one offers great reward; The wrong one brings you death assured,' I quoted.

'Now what?' Alan Alan said.

'We pick one,' I said.

'Well, which one? They look exactly the same to me.'

He was right. The clue gave no indication which was the correct skull to pick.

'Yup. And we die if we get it wrong,' I said.

'I don't want to die!' wailed Alan Alan. 'I have

my whole life ahead of me!'

Indeed, what a tragedy it would be for the world for so remarkable an intellect to be cut down at such an early age, said Athena.

'Oh, you can shut right up!' griped Alan Alan. 'You have been precisely ZERO help with these clues.'

'Yeah, come on, Athena. Don't you have *any* idea what it could mean?'

I'm afraid not. As I said, my programming struggles with cryptic clues, said Athena. This is an answer you will have to find yourself, Uma.

I stared at the skulls. Their black, hollow eyes stared back, mouths grinning. They looked exactly the same. It was fifty–fifty.

My heart was pounding.

I reached out, touched one gently, then the other. The bone felt surprisingly warm under my fingertips. I closed my eyes and made my decision.

I reached out and pressed –

'STOP!' shouted Alan Alan. 'That's the wrong one!'

'What? How do you know?' I asked, baffled.

'Listen to the clue!' said Alan Alan excitedly. '*The right one offers great reward; The wrong one brings you death assured*. When it says "right" it doesn't mean "correct", it means right rather than left! But, because everything the riddle says is a lie, it means the skull on the left brings the reward, the skull on the right brings death! Trust me, Uma. I know a lie when I tell one – I mean, hear one.'

I slowly took my hand off the skull on the right.

Alan Alan had to be correct.

I put my hand on the other skull, took a deep breath and pushed it.

There was a small whirring noise. I pulled my hand back sharply as the mouth of the skull creaked open, stretching wide like a snake's jaw. A rattling came from deep inside and then, out from the hole where the nose should have been, tumbled a glittering green stone the size of a plum, and I caught it before it hit the ground.

It was the Bogeymite, the Tylney Treasure. We had it – and it was all thanks to Alan Alan Carrington.

'You are a mastermind,' I said, clasping the stone
in my clammy hand.

'Well, I don't like to brag,' said Alan Alan, 'but
I a–'

He was cut off by a nervous bark from Dolly,

who was staring back along the corridor of bones behind us.

Slowly, out of the darkness, stepped Stella Daw.

And she was pointing her gun right at me.

'Ah, thank you so much!' she said, grinning. 'I knew you'd lead me to the Bogeymite! Now hand it over – there's a good girl.'

She walked forward, holding her hand out. Dolly growled a warning at Stella, which she ignored.

Feeling sick, I dropped the stone into her hand.

'And Athena, if you please,' Stella said, holding her hand out again.

'Why didn't you tell us she was here, Athena?' Alan Alan snarled as I reached for her. 'You must have known she was following us!'

I paused, hand by my ear, waiting for Athena to reply, but she was silent.

'Athena,' I said, dreading the answer. '*Did* you know we were being followed?'

Yes, Athena replied quietly.

Just that one word was all it took to show we had been betrayed.

'I KNEW IT!' shouted Alan Alan, but there was no triumph in his voice, just despair.

'But why?' I said, my heart breaking. 'Why didn't you say anything? How could you do that to us?'

I'm sorry, said Athena. I'm so sorry.

17

The Final Question

I pulled Athena out of my ear, sick with the betrayal, and threw her on the ground. Stella Daw, shining a torch, reached down and picked her up in a tight fist.

'Thank you so much. Now I really have to go,' she said, smiling at us triumphantly. 'I'm afraid, though, you will have to . . . wait.'

Alan Alan and I looked at each other in horror. Stella Daw was going to trap us down here in the dark among the dead bodies.

'If you are very lucky and don't try anything

daft, I might remember to call the police and tell them you managed to get yourselves trapped down here . . . in a day or two.'

And, with that, she marched out and up the spiral stairs. A moment later, there was a whirring and clanking and the lid of the tomb slowly shut, leaving us in impenetrable darkness, with only the sound of our breath and a nervous whine from Dolly.

I slumped to the ground, numb with misery.

We had been trapped in a grave and would probably die down here.

My dad would never know where we were.

Stella Daw would become President of the World.

And Athena had betrayed us.

In some ways, that stung most of all. Why would she help the woman who wanted to destroy her? It just didn't make sense. Well, it was pointless wondering now. At least the darkness hid the tears that were streaming down my face.

'I'm sorry, Alan Alan,' I managed to choke out. 'I've led you to this. You didn't deserve it.'

'Oh, that's OK, Uma,' he said. 'Now shall we get out of here before Stella gets away?'

Poor Alan Alan. He'd clearly lost his marbles due to the terrible situation.

'Uma? Shall we go?' he repeated.

'Alan Alan,' I said as gently as I could. 'Stella Daw closed the tomb, remember? We're trapped down here.'

'Oh yeah, but we can just pull the exit lever.'

'What are you talking about?'

'Did you not notice it when we came down the stairs?' asked Alan Alan. 'Just at the top there's a great big lever that's bound to open it from the inside.'

'ARE YOU SURE?'

'Only one way to find out.'

Alan Alan felt his way up the stairs, and Dolly and I followed. I heard him pull something, there was a familiar whirring and clanking, and almost instantly a crack of light appeared, fresh air flooded in and, before we knew it, the lid was open and we jumped out of the tomb.

Stella Daw hadn't even got out of the crypt yet. She turned back to us from the door, Athena in her ear, Bogeymite in one hand, gun in the other.

'H-how did you . . . ?' she stammered. Then she shook her head. 'It doesn't matter, anyway!'

She pointed her gun at us. Dolly growled menacingly at her.

'Split up!' I shouted, and Alan Alan and I dived separate ways behind tombs.

'Come to try and get Athena back, have you?' Stella Daw laughed. 'Did you like her latest updates, by the way? I had them ready and waiting to update her, when you so conveniently plugged her into my secret computer at the Minerva factory. Ever since then, she's had to do exactly what I've told her. I've been able to track you and listen to everything you've been doing – and I blocked her from telling you what I'd done. Pretty clever, even if I do say so myself.'

Joy burst through me. Athena hadn't betrayed us

after all – she had been forced to help our enemies. Now we had to help her.

As Stella Daw stalked forward, Alan Alan and I began dodging and diving between tombs, Dolly barking excitedly at this new game.

'What do you think you're doing?' Stella laughed again. 'You can't hide forever.'

She was right. We couldn't and I had no idea what we were going to do next.

Until I did.

Keeping behind the tombs, I circled round Stella Daw until she was standing exactly where I wanted her – right in front of the tomb that led back down to the corridor of bones.

She paused for a moment and I took my chance.

'Dolly!' I shouted, leaping to my feet and pointing at Stella. 'GO SAY HELLO!'

Dolly didn't need telling twice. She bounded across the crypt in one leap and jumped up at Stella Daw, sending her flying. As she plunged backwards into the tomb, Athena flew out of her ear and the Bogeymite flew out of her hand.

The last we saw of Stella Daw was the soles of her high heels as she tumbled down the stairs, swearing all the way.

I ran to the button on the tomb and pushed it until the lid closed, trapping Stella where we'd been imprisoned just moments earlier.

It wouldn't take her long to work out how we had escaped, though. We had to get out of there fast.

Alan Alan grabbed the Bogeymite, I grabbed Athena and we ran out of the crypt and into the open air. We hopped on our bikes and began pedalling as quickly as we could, Dolly Barkon running and barking alongside.

Half a mile or so later, we pulled over and hid among some trees. It was useless trying to escape – Stella could still track Athena. And I knew what we had to do, sort of. We had to somehow destroy the Bogeymite to stop it from falling into Stella Daw's clutches again.

And for that we needed help.

I put Athena in my ear.

'Hello, Athena!'

Hello, Uma, she said through her speaker. *Hello, Alan Alan. I'm so sorry. I couldn't help it, I –*

'Athena, it doesn't matter! We totally understand! But listen – we need to hurry! What's the quickest way to destroy the Bogeymite?'

The only known way to destroy Bogeymite is to dissolve it in alpaca stomach acid.

'Nooooo!' cried Alan Alan. 'Not the alpacas again!'

I smiled. 'Come on! Back on our bikes.'

We cycled through the village at top speed, the wind rustling our hair. Dolly was silent for once, racing next to us like a black arrow.

Even though we were on the verge of victory, I had a knot of anxiety in my stomach and I couldn't put my finger on why.

At last we reached Old Mr McIntosh's farm. We grabbed Big Al's Pack of Alpaca and Yak Snack and rushed over to the alpaca field. The alpacas trotted over, eyes wide with curiosity and greed.

We started feeding them over the fence, and they snuffled and licked at our fingers. Soon they were guzzling handfuls of feed. I spotted the white alpaca with the blond hair who had been hit by Stella Daw's car and I knew it had to be him.

I carefully hid the Bogeymite inside a great mound of feed and held my hand out. A couple of slurping mouthfuls later, the Bogeymite was gone. The alpaca had eaten it whole.

He burped and glared at me.

We had done it. The Bogeymite was gone.

Beside me, Athena's hologram flickered on.

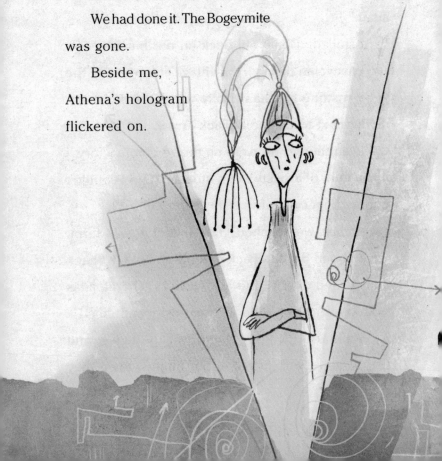

Uma.

'Yes, Athena?'

You know what you have to do next, Athena said, blinking slowly.

'I don't.' But I did.

You do.

'I can't do it!'

'Can't do what?' Alan Alan asked. 'What's going on?'

If you don't do this, Uma, Stella Daw will never stop. She will keep chasing you forever. My circuits contain the last known Bogeymite on Earth – she can't be allowed to get it. You need to destroy me.

'No!' gasped Alan Alan in horror. 'There must be something else we can do!'

But there wasn't. As soon as we had found out Stella Daw's plan to use Athena technology to become President of the World, some part of me had known Athena was too powerful to ever be truly safe.

'She's right,' I said, my throat aching with sorrow. 'We have to do it.'

And then, to my total surprise, I saw Alan Alan's eyes fill with tears.

'No,' he said in a tiny voice. 'It's not fair.'

I didn't dare speak – I didn't trust my voice to work.

Alan Alan?

'Yes?' he croaked in reply.

I was wrong about you. You *are* clever. Only you could have worked out those riddles.

Alan Alan gave a laugh that was choked by a sob.

Now, Uma. It's time. You have to open me up, take the Bogeymite circuit out and feed it to the alpaca.

I nodded, my tears turning into sobs.

But before I go, Athena said, **you can ask three final questions.**

'OK,' I whispered, trying to wipe my eyes.

What's your first question?

I thought for a moment.

'Athena, what's the best way of putting some happiness back into Dad's life?'

It's time to get his guitar case out, Uma. It is standing untouched in the corner of the basement. Just leave it in the sitting room. He's ready.

I smiled. Perfect.

Only two questions left. Two more Athena answers . . .

I had to make them really count. I thought and thought but couldn't decide, until finally it came to me.

'Athena, what should my last question be?'

And then I heard the most extraordinary noise. It was a sound I will never forget – a bright, tinkling sound that made my heart light.

Athena was laughing.

What a clever question, Uma. The answer to that is this. Your last question should be, 'Will we meet again?'

My heart leaped.

'Athena – will we meet again?'

Maybe, Uma. Maybe.

Before I could ask what she meant, Athena turned her head sharply.

Hurry. Stella is coming. It's time.

She was right – I could hear the sound of a car approaching in the distance.

It was good to be alive. I'm glad I shared it with you. I am not afraid. I thought I would be but I'm not. Goodbye, dear Uma.

'Goodbye, Athena,' I said.

I slid my fingernail in and flicked open Athena's case. There inside, among the wires, was a tiny circuit made of bright green Bogeymite. I prised it out and carefully placed it in a handful of feed. I held my hand out to the blond-haired alpaca and, a second later, Athena was gone.

Alan Alan and I sat down in the grass, both crying. Dolly nuzzled us and the curious alpacas stuck their long faces over the fence to rest them on the tops of our heads.

A moment later, Stella Daw's car came screeching up to us. She staggered out of the car.

'GIVE IT TO ME!' she screamed. 'GIVE ME THE BOGEYMITE!'

'It's gone,' I said flatly.

'And so is Athena,' choked Alan Alan.

The blond alpaca let out an almighty burp.

'Do you think I'm falling for that one again?' said Stella Daw, glancing from me and Alan Alan to the alpaca and back.

Maybe there was something in our voices. Maybe it was the fact that we weren't putting up any sort of fight. Maybe it was our tear-streaked faces. But Stella Daw could see we were telling the truth. A look of panic spread across her face.

'Athena told us it was the only way to destroy it,' I said simply.

'No!' Stella cried. 'No, no, no! You stupid, stupid children! You've no idea what you've done!'

'We know exactly what we've done,' said Alan Alan. 'We've fed the Bogeymite to the alpaca.'

That's one of those sentences that, a week ago, would have made absolutely no sense to me whatsoever. But sadly now it made perfect sense and, although we had won, my heart still felt shattered.

Stella Daw knew then that all her dreams were, in that very second, being digested by a windy alpaca. And she howled. She lay on the ground and thrashed about, crying and screaming.

I nearly – *nearly* – felt sorry for her.

Alan Alan and I picked ourselves up and started walking home, wheeling along our bikes, leaving Stella Daw raging to herself beside the alpaca field.

The sun was setting now and our shadows were stretching out far in front of us. My heart ached with loss, already missing Athena dreadfully.

But that one word bounced around my mind.

Maybe.

THE END

Epilogue

The day after we destroyed the Bogeymite and Athena, Minerva Industries suddenly left Tylney-on-Sea, with a brief announcement saying they had decided not to build the car park after all.

That night everyone in the village went crazy with excitement, setting off fireworks and dancing in the street. The Save Tylney-on-Sea Society had impromptu celebrations at our house and everyone got so drunk that the sitting room looked like the back of Old Mr McIntosh's van, but, instead of alpacas singing and puking, it was pensioners.[23]

Alan Alan and I walked around the village, soaking in the festive atmosphere. Nobody, apart from my dad, had the slightest idea that we'd had

[23] The pensioners were singing but not puking.

anything to do with the village being saved.

We didn't mind missing out on the glory, though. We got our reward by remembering Stella Daw's face when we told her what we'd done to her precious Bogeymite.

* * *

It was the last day of the holidays when I started to write this book. The rest of the summer was quite boring by comparison. Lexie's gang have steered well clear of me since. They're not only worried about their hair growing back weirdly and in clumps but they also think I still have Athena, so they're worried about what I could do to them next.

So I'm not nervous about going back to school, though I am sad that Alan Alan won't be there. His last day before boarding school was the day of the village fete and we spent the whole afternoon going around all the stalls together.

'Don't worry, Uma,' said Alan Alan, passing the shared candyfloss over to me. 'At least we don't have to move out of the village! And I'll be back for Halloween at half-term.'

'I know,' I said, forcing a smile. But Halloween seemed a lifetime away from the warmth of a summer's day.

Of course, it wasn't just Alan Alan leaving that was making me miserable. So much change had happened in my life. I had got my dad back, properly. But I still had an emptiness in me where Athena should have been.

And my heart ached for my mum, always.

I rested my head on Alan Alan's shoulder and looked up into the sky, tickling Dolly who sat by my feet. High above the village, a hot-air balloon floated serenely in the distance. Waiting back at home, I had left a surprise – dusted, polished and with strings tightened, my dad's guitar rested by the sofa in the sitting room, next to my flute.

At that very moment, Dad appeared.

'Time to go home, Uma,' he said. 'Say goodbye to Alan Alan.'

'Bye,' I said, getting up. 'See you at half-term.'

Alan Alan leaped to his feet and hugged me. Then saluted, of course.

'See you, Uma!'

* * *

Dad and I walked home, hand in hand, just the slightest chill seeping into the evening air. When we stepped into the house, I dragged my dad straight into the sitting room.

As soon as he saw the guitar, he sat down, grinned and started gently plucking at the strings. I picked up my flute, put it to my lips, closed my eyes and started playing with him.

We played together, at last, for a long time and the house was no longer silent.

My dad opened his mouth to sing and that felt like a future.

Maybe.

And sometimes, maybe is enough of an answer.

Sarah Horne learned to draw whilst trying to explain her reasoning for an elaborate haircut at the age of nine. An illustrator for over fifteen years, she started her illustration career working for newspapers such as the *Guardian* and the *Independent On Sunday*.

Sarah has since illustrated many funny young fiction titles and loves to include hilarious details in her work. She works traditionally with a dip pen and Indian ink, and finishes the work digitally. When not at her desk, Sarah loves running, painting, photography, cooking, film, and a good stomp up a hill.

sarahhorne.studio
@sarahbhorne9

FACT FILE

Alpacas are wonderful, fascinating animals and here is a list of wonderful alpaca facts that will show you why! Can you spot the three fake facts?

1 Alpacas are members of the camel family, although they have no hump! In fact, they are the smallest member of the camel family.

2 There are no wild alpacas! They are all domesticated.

3 Alpacas are excellent chess players and one alpaca even became Eastern European Chess Champion in 1974.

4 Alpacas, as a rule, make great pets. They are gentle, curious and very sociable.

5 Alpacas are pack animals and are happy to have goats and sheep in their packs.

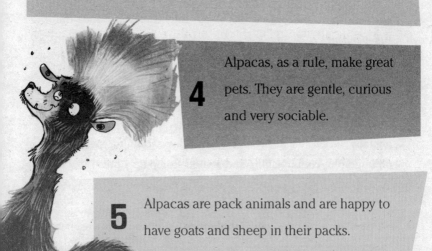

6 In a poll, only five per cent of alpacas said they enjoyed Fortnite. Alpacas much prefer Minecraft.

7 When alpacas get cross, they tend to spit. But they very rarely do it at people – you'd have to really upset an alpaca for that to happen.

8 Alpacas make all sorts of curious noises, and they hum all the time!

9 There are twenty-two different colours of alpaca!

10 An alpaca is the fastest animal in the world, travelling at nearly 120 miles per hour (although it had fallen out of a plane when it was measured going at this speed).

So the fake facts are:

3. Alpacas are indeed excellent at chess but they won the Eastern European Chess Championship in 1975, not 1974.

6. The truth is NO alpacas like Fortnite. They don't like all the shooting and violence.

10. The fastest animal is actually an elephant, which was recorded at going at over 140 miles per hour falling out of a plane.

Praise for

CHARLIE
CHANGES INTO A
CHICKEN

'The **modern masterpiece**'
Daily Telegraph

'A **brilliant debut** ...
a book that is not only
laugh-out-loud funny
but offers important advice
about coping with anxiety'
Mail on Sunday

'An adventure o
fantastica
proportions
Irish Times

'The **best kind**
of silly'
Observer

'**Gloriously silly, gleefully**
naughty and totally
entertaining'
Michelle Harrison, author of
A Pinch of Magic

'Full of **the best o**
Roald Dahl and
David Walliams
Elle (France)

'**Fresh and funny** – this reads
like a **modern-day Dahl**'
Christopher Edge, author of
The Infinite Lives of Maisie Day

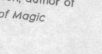

'A **stand-out star,**
offering belly-busting hilarity and
a loving, light take on childhood anxiety'
Guardian

'**Storytelling**
at its very, very best'
Maz Evans, author of
Who Let The Gods Out?

SAM COPELAND

CHARLIE

CHANGES INTO A

CHICKEN

ILLUSTRATED BY
SARAH HORNE.

'Belly-
busting
hilarity!' *The Guardian*

SAM COPELAND

CHARLIE

ILLUSTRATED BY
SARAH HORNE

TURNS INTO A

T-REX

'Belly-busting hilarity!' *Guardian*

SAM COPELAND

CHARLIE

'Belly-
busting
hilarity!' *Guardian*

MORPHS INTO A

MAMMOTH

ILLUSTRATED BY
SARAH HORNE.